— Jenny looked around, chilled by what she saw. Josh's room. A mess. Mounds of clothes slung across the backs of chairs, gym socks hanging out dresser drawers, cleats and sneakers in the middle of the floor, baseball posters with curling corners thumbtacked to the walls. . . .

— And then the horror deepened, oozing through every pore of her being.

— She stared down at what she expected to be herself, only to find she had been moved into Josh Friedman's body!

— Unbelievable. Totally. Jenny slid out of bed, feeling unusually clumsy, and padded across the room to the mirror that hung over the dresser. Above the clutter of books and paints and surfing paraphernalia, Josh's face stared back at her from the glass. Jenny ran her fingers over the face frantically. . . .

— Don't panic, she told herself. You'll wake up and everything will be fine.

**Other Point paperbacks
you will enjoy:**

Changing Places

Susan Smith

SCHOLASTIC INC.
New York Toronto London Auckland Sydney

For my dear friend, Marilyn Kaye

*For your careful attention and advice,
a special thank you, Ted Stevenson.*

ISBN 0-590-33580-4

12 11 10 9 8 7 6 5   8 9/8 0 1/9

Printed in the U.S.A.   01

First Scholastic printing, December 1986

Chapter 1

Jenny Knudson felt a light tap on her shoulder. She turned around in her seat to meet Josh Friedman's sea-green eyes. As much as she knew she should be concentrating on the lecture, she couldn't control the rush of love that swamped her at the sight of Josh's tanned, smiling face.

His forefinger caught one of her red-brown curls and twirled it lazily. "Wanna go for a Coke after class?" he whispered.

Jenny wagged her head no — she would explain to him after class. When she faced the front of the room again, their English teacher, Mr. Burns, was staring directly at her.

"Unless you want to share your discussion with the entire class, Ms. Knudson and Mr. Friedman, I suggest you pay attention," Mr. Burns reprimanded in an icy tone.

Jenny held her breath, concentrating on how Mr. Burns's eyebrows bobbed up and down as though controlled by puppet strings.

They seemed separate from the rest of his face.

"Another thing to remember, you two, is that 'attention' rhymes with 'detention'." A wry smile parted Mr. Burns's thin lips.

"Geez," John hissed beneath his breath, but only Jenny heard him.

A flicker of annoyance with Josh passed through her. She wished he didn't always try to make contact with her in class — he must know how it distracted her. Had he forgotten that she couldn't afford to stay after school this Wednesday, especially now, with an audition for the summer session of a major ballet school coming up soon? Her dance instructor, Mrs. Herbert, had selected five top students to audition at a San Francisco school, and was working closely with the special group to prepare them for it. Getting into the school would be a major step in Jenny's dancing career. So it was dance every day after school now and a dress rehearsal on Saturday.

Jenny's stomach twisted into a hard knot as she thought. Dance meant everything to her. While dancing, she forgot herself completely, pulled up into a tornado of separateness and indescribable pleasure. But Josh didn't understand that. Sure, he understood his *own* brand of dedication but not hers.

Now he tugged at the end of her hair, but she ignored him. She couldn't take the chance of speaking to him now that Mr. Burns had his eye on them, so she tried to concentrate on the lecture.

They were discussing Franz Kafka's *Metamorphosis*. Jenny tried to imagine how it would be to wake up and discover yourself in an insect's body instead of your own. The author made it seem really possible, and Jenny found herself identifying with the man to whom it happened in the story.

When the bell rang, Josh gave Jenny's hair a playful tug. She turned around.

"Finally, I get your full attention." He leaned forward, his face within inches of hers, as though he were about to kiss her. Then he pulled away.

"Is that what you want?" she asked.

"Well, sure. Shouldn't I?"

Jenny scooped up her books and stood beside him. She was petite and delicate-looking; a slender, almost thin body, and long legs and arms. Mrs. Herbert had once told her she had the perfect dancer's build. Jenny's eyes were brown, and her creamy complexion made a nice contrast with her rich auburn hair.

Next to Josh, Jenny felt tiny. By comparison, Josh was tall, lanky — all muscle and energy. Sports were the perfect medium for him. He played baseball with a natural ease, and sometimes it was maddening to Jenny to find that he excelled, seemingly without effort.

Josh's seal-brown hair dipped over a pair

of contrite green eyes. "Hey, I know something's bugging you. What gives?"

They walked out of the class, Josh's arm around her waist. Just his touch sparked something deep within Jenny. Sometimes, it was so disturbing to her, she wished he wouldn't touch her because her most important thoughts would scatter like beads sprung loose from a necklace. How could he do that to her, she wondered. Yet sometimes, met with Josh's wide-eyed puzzlement, she was aware that she had a similar effect on him.

Once they were in the hall, she answered him. "I was annoyed at you for bugging me in class. I mean, who needs detention, Josh?"

"Nobody needs it. It's a waste of time. But I just knew Burns wouldn't give it to us. We're good students," he explained.

"That's not the point. I have an audition coming up in two weeks and I can't afford to miss one single minute of dance rehearsal until then." Jenny sighed, brushing her reddish-brown hair over one shoulder. It touched her waist in a series of rippling waves that Josh loved to spread his fingers through.

"Look, I'm sorry, Jenny, okay? I didn't mean to get you in trouble. I wasn't thinking about your dance class. I was just thinking. . . ." He waited until she turned to gaze at him, then blasted her with his full, all-star smile. "About you."

"You're such a charmer," she laughed,

knowing she had flushed crimson. It was hard to stay mad at him. "But I love you."

"I love you, too." Josh moved ahead to Jenny's locker. "So, how about that Coke? You must have a few minutes before dance class."

"Josh, you know I'd love to, but I have just about enough time to pull on a leotard, grab an orange, and leave for the studio. You know what my schedule's like."

"Do I!" he exclaimed, watching her open her locker and pick three books to take home. "I only wish there was room in it for me."

"Don't pout. I try, Josh, I really try. I mean, I really wish my schedule wasn't like this, too. When I've got time, I'm all yours, okay? I'd rather be with you than with anyone else in the whole world."

"Yeah, I know." He lightly kicked her locker door, sounding unconvinced. "So my only competition is a stretch leotard, right?"

Jenny laughed. "I could say the same thing about your baseball team."

"No, I don't think so. The baseball team is a thrill, but I've never let a bat and glove get between us." He kissed her, full on the lips. Jenny shivered at the sensation tripping through her.

She knew she could easily lose herself in Josh, but she was afraid of giving up a part of herself in the process. It was easy to imagine concentrating solely on him, as a lot of girls did with their boyfriends. But something wouldn't let her, even though she felt that the excitement he stirred in her was enough to sustain her for a long time. (She didn't want to think "forever," because that was expecting a lot of anyone, including herself.)

Dance helped Jenny keep her balance about a lot of things in her life, not Josh. For instance, when her mother had been in the hospital, Jenny had plunged into dancing with a fervor that had given her the strength to deal with that frightening situation.

"Let me come with you, Jenny. Maybe I can help," Josh said.

"Help me do what?" Jenny blinked, still lost in her own thoughts.

"Help you get home, help you change, help you peel your orange. . . ." He grinned. She smiled and squeezed his hand. Practice every day after school. . . . Was she becoming a bore to Josh with all this dancing? She hoped not, and yet the fear that she might be turning him off kept nagging at her.

But like most boys she'd known, Josh had a way of not seeing both sides of a problem. She often felt he knew what *he* wanted, but that he didn't take *her* feelings seriously. Right now, he was making her feel really guilty, and he didn't even know it.

They strolled out of the school building, in the direction of Jenny's house. Under a maple tree, Josh plucked off a green leaf and stroked Jenny's cheek with it, as though outlining her bone structure. The gesture brought to mind the freestyle sketches of trees and birds she'd seen in Josh's room once. She thought he was talented in art, but he considered himself a mere doodler.

Jenny was the first to break the mood, even though the gentle scratch of the leaf felt nice. "We'd better get going," she said, her hand moving to her face to take his hand.

"There just aren't enough hours in a day for you, are there, Jen?" Josh asked, looking disappointed.

"No. I've been thinking of renting extras," she said, laughing.

As they walked up the path to Jenny's house, Josh slipped behind her, grabbed her around the waist, and carried her kicking and screaming, into the lawn sprinklers.

"Josh . . . put me down! Honestly, can't you be more serious?" Jenny cried, yet she was unable to keep the laughter out of her voice. By the time she wriggled free of his grasp, she was soaking wet and her clothing was clinging to her. Her tennis shoes were covered with damp grass clippings. Josh stood by and grinned.

"We'll have to leave our shoes outside the door," she said.

"Okay by me." Josh followed her inside the spacious, two-story house. Jenny's room was in the attic — the most remote room in the house. The best part about it was the view: a vast lawn that sloped into deep woods. The room had an airy atmosphere and was decorated with dance posters and pink-

and-white pillows that matched the walls. Another great feature was the window seat in front of the triangular window, which was barely big enough for two people.

Josh sat down on the window seat and pulled Jenny onto his lap.

He leaned his head back and she kissed him, his arms, meanwhile, tightening around her waist. Jenny didn't resist. It was springtime. A weightlessness overtook her and she was floating like a helium balloon. Bright rivers of sunlight coated the two of them in warmth. She wanted the kiss to go on forever. She wasn't sure she wanted to go to the studio this afternoon. That was how Josh distracted her, causing her feelings to collide. . . .

Suddenly, Josh slipped his hand up inside Jenny's blouse. It felt nice, but Jenny firmly pushed his hand back down to her waist, where it had been before.

"Come on, Jen," Josh kissed her hair.

"No. I have to get dressed." She slid off his lap and tucked in her blouse, even though two seconds later she would take everything off after Josh left the room.

Josh held Jenny by her little finger. His face was flushed, his eyes dark, with either anger or disappointment, or a mixture of both. Jenny didn't know — she didn't always understand him.

She moved completely away from him, suddenly frightened of the power of her own feelings for him. She felt her control slip when he kissed her, accompanied by some nameless need to protect herself.

"Look at the time," she said. "I've got to change. I can't be late." She motioned to the red digital clock by her bed. There was barely enough time to get her leotard on and bike over to Mrs. Herbert's dance studio.

"Okay." Reluctantly, Josh rose and crossed the room. He closed the door quietly behind him.

Jenny changed into a red leotard and black tights, hastily threw on a warm-up suit over her dance clothes, and put her worn ballet slippers in a canvas bag. Lastly, she pushed a sweatband down over her reddish-brown hair and went to find Josh.

He was in the den, playing a video game on the computer. He heard her come in but didn't look up. Jenny guessed he was giving her the silent treatment, which she couldn't stand.

"Talk to me, Josh." Jenny watched the game over his shoulder. Pac Man gobbled up ghosts in fast succession.

"Wait." He racked up a hefty score. "Finished." Josh turned to face her. "Sometimes, Jenny . . . sometimes I just want you so much, I don't think straight. I forget about time, dancing, even baseball."

Jenny smiled. "Well, it happens to me, too, only in a different way, I think."

"Yeah?"

"Yeah. But I don't have time to explain."

"Okay. Well, we'll be together after my

game on Saturday," Josh said, as though consoling himself with this fact. He got up and slid his arms around her waist, pulling her toward him.

"Game? This Saturday?" Jenny gulped. Josh's big play-off baseball game. She'd forgotten it would be this weekend.

"Well, sure. You knew about it. I've been telling you it was coming up for a couple of months now." Josh kissed her and nuzzled her ear.

"Yes, but I didn't think it was so soon." Jenny didn't have the heart to tell him it had slipped her mind. She had known about the game. She wasn't able to go to many of his games, but she'd promised to attend this most important one.

"I've got a dance rehearsal," she managed weakly.

Josh dropped his hands to his sides, his passion suddenly cooled. "No kidding? Did you arrange it specially for Saturday?"

"It's been scheduled for a long time. It never occurred to me that both things were on the same day. It's the only dress run we're going to have. I'm sorry," Jenny apologized.

"Oh, it's okay. Just fine. The big play-off of the year, and your girl friend doesn't even show up to cheer for you." He sounded bitter.

Jenny placed her hand on his shoulder, wanting so much to comfort him. "Josh, don't." Fear fluttered in her chest as his body tensed at her touch. She wished he wouldn't do that. He walled her off, just with his body language. "Look, I'll do my best, okay? Rehearsal will probably be over around five. Maybe I can make the last inning." She knew that was pushing it, but she wanted to ease his disappointment.

"Yeah, sure."

Jenny was vaguely aware of the flickering computer screen behind Josh, which tinged his features green.

"We can go out afterward — just the two of us," she went on, hopefully. He didn't answer. Her words thudded uselessly against the wall of his anger.

"Sometimes, I really wonder if you love me, Jenny," he said softly.

The words stung her. "Then you are blind, and maybe stupid," she shot back, ready to burst into tears. Why did they have to fight like this? And right before a class, too.

"My game isn't important to you, Jen. Let's face it, what you want to do comes first. Me second."

"That's not true!" Jenny cried. "You wouldn't give up your play-off just to watch me in a recital, would you?"

He frowned. "Probably not, but this is a sign of the way we are. Hardly ever together."

He gazed at the parquet floor, the computer screen's green glow picking out the highlights in his hair. "I just wish you could walk around in my shoes for a while, Jen. Then maybe you'd understand how I feel."

11

"Oh, really? Well, the feeling's mutual, Josh. I wish *you* could walk around in *mine*."

"I beg your pardon," an unfamiliar voice intoned.

Jenny and Josh jerked to attention. Simultaneously, they whirled around, looking for the source of the intruding voice.

They stared at the computer screen, where a man's face was clearly featured. He didn't smile, but gazed at them, as though assessing each of them carefully. Lines webbed outward from a pair of knowing gray eyes to touch a salt-and-pepper hairline. There was something vaguely unsettling about his rough facial features.

"Your wish is granted," the man on the screen said. His voice was rich, mellifluous, and moved over Jenny's senses like warm water. When Josh turned to look at her, she realized by his shocked expression that he was just as startled as she was.

"Who are you and where'd you come from?" demanded Josh, striding over to the computer. Furiously, he punched keys, then ran his hands over the screen.

"Hey, no use trying to blow my circuits." The man held up his long-fingered hand. Jenny was struck by the strangeness of his palm. He had a lifeline that traveled through the center of it, then continued, unbroken along the outside edge. "I operate on a different frequency. No ROM and RAM for me, no bits and bytes. Frankly, I don't understand them."

"Then how did you get inside that screen?" Josh wanted to know. He stared intently at the picture, straining to understand what was happening.

"Oh, it's such a tedious story that I don't want to bother you with it. But I repeat, your wish is granted."

"Wish?" Jenny blinked.

"Your wish to be in each other's shoes," he explained simply.

"Oh, give me a break," Josh rolled his eyes in disbelief. He turned to Jenny. "This guy can't be for real. I mean, there are some pretty strange kooks in this town, but this guy really takes the cake, doesn't he?"

"Yes," Jenny answered uncertainly.

"At least we agree on *something*," Josh said with sarcasm.

"I assure you, I'm no kook," the man on the screen said firmly. "I have a certain power. . . ."

"You could easily fool us," Josh said.

Jenny stifled a nervous giggle. Josh paced back and forth across the room. The man on the screen shrugged, as though Josh's words didn't really faze him.

"Who are you, anyway?" Jenny asked.

He stared directly at Josh. "Your fairy godfather."

"No kidding?" Josh cried, shaking his head in sheer disbelief. "I don't believe this. Are you mine, or Jenny's?"

"I'm here for the sake of both of you."

"Nice, real nice," Josh said as he ran a

forefinger over the computer keyboard.

"You sure are weird," Jenny observed. "Nobody believes in fairy godfathers nowadays."

"Outdated stuff, huh?" the man asked.

"Well, yeah. You'd do better to say you were from outer space," she told him.

"I'll take that into consideration." The man's face remained serious, a mask of sorts. Josh and Jenny exchanged glances and laughed. "The fact remains," he continued, "that your wish is granted. You will spend some time in each other's shoes."

Josh chuckled. "And when is this supposed to take place?"

"Tomorrow morning," the man replied in a solemn tone.

"Right. Okay. How will we know when it's happening?" Josh stood in front of the screen now, his arm linked through Jenny's. She stroked his hand absently, a little fearful all of a sudden.

"You will awaken, and the trade will have already taken place. The exchange will last exactly three days."

"You're putting a spell on us," Jenny concluded jokingly, trying to ease the tension that seemed to fill the room.

"In a manner of speaking, yes." The man's image flickered.

Was he signing off? Jenny wondered.

"I don't believe this guy, Jen." Josh gave her hand a firm squeeze.

"You *will* believe me," the man said, with

rather chilling confidence. There was the hint of a smile on his lips.

Jenny was just about to ask him if he had a name, when he disappeared. Vanished. Josh ran forward and touched the screen and keyboard.

"Remember, he's on a different wavelength," Jenny reminded him.

Josh whirled around. "Did you set this up, Jen?"

"Me! Now, how would I think up anything quite that crazy?" Her canvas bag dropped to her feet and she bent to pick it up.

"You don't know anything about this?" he pressed.

"Of course not. I'm just as surprised as you are."

Josh studied her thoughtfully, his seagreen eyes boring into hers. "Wow. Then did you see what I saw?"

"I hope not." Jenny closed her eyes, recapturing the strange man's face in her memory. The conversation, if it could be called that, had taken place in a matter of minutes. Certainly, it had been weird. Even in the twentieth century, with all its available technology, it had seemed unearthly.

Josh checked the computer one more time before leaving the room.

Outside in the hall, Jenny shivered as Josh took her hand.

"Well, do you think it's really going to happen? What he said, I mean?"

Josh laughed. "Are you serious? Naw, it's

just one of those freak things. Like a UFO landing. Two people see it, try to talk everyone into believing it, but nobody ever does. So what's the sense of even reporting it to anyone? It's just a shared, but unbelievable, experience."

Jenny grinned at him. "Is this the kind of shared experience you were looking for, Josh?"

He laughed softly. "Not exactly, Jen. This one never entered my mind. Maybe we dreamed the whole thing."

"Maybe." Jenny was remembering the man's richly textured voice, the unnatural lifeline, and half a dozen books she'd read on people turning into other things and technology taking over the world. Creating monsters. Turning humans into robots.

This guy had been *real*. There was nothing unreal about him, except for the fact that he turned up on a computer screen, out of absolutely nowhere.

Chapter 2

It was Thursday morning, and Jenny knew something was different before she even opened her eyes. Unfamiliar sounds and vaguely familiar voices met her ears. Though she couldn't pinpoint exactly *what* was different, she found her mind trying to shape the information it received into a logical pattern.

A breeze moved over her from the opposite direction than was usual. The window across her room was generally opened halfway, and the wind would ruffle the papers on her desk.

But no papers rattled. Her body felt heavy, achey, as though she might be getting the flu. But different.

Light footsteps sounded on the other side of the door. She heard an insistent rap and then, "Josh, get up! It's eight-fifteen!"

Jenny's eyes flew open. Did someone say *Josh?* She stared at a pale green ceiling — not her own. She wasn't in her own room.

Then she looked around, chilled by what

she saw. Josh's room. A mess. Mounds of clothes slung across the backs of chairs, gym socks hanging out of dresser drawers, cleats and sneakers in the middle of the floor, baseball posters with curling corners thumbtacked to the walls.

Jenny lay in Josh's bed and let these images assault her for a moment before yanking back the covers. And then the horror deepened, oozing through every pore of her being.

She stared down at what she expected to be herself, only to find she had been moved into Josh Friedman's body!

"No!" she cried out in disbelief. She looked and looked at this body until her eyes ached.

Unbelievable, totally. Jenny slid out of bed, feeling unusually clumsy, and padded across the room to the mirror that hung over the dresser. Above the clutter of books and paints and surfing paraphernalia, Josh's face stared back at her from the glass. Jenny ran her fingers over the face frantically, desperately, expecting any minute now she would wake up from a bad dream.

Don't panic, she told herself. You'll wake up and everything will be fine. It's just because of that silly man in the computer screen, claiming to be your fairy godfather. Of all crazy things. Of course, none of this is real.

Jenny slumped into a chair, trying to calm herself down. Minutes ticked away, but nothing changed. Nothing, absolutely nothing. What was happening? She focused on the dark straight hair on Josh's arms, waiting for her own arms to replace his. Like in werewolf movies, when the werewolf turns back into a man at dawn.

She located Josh's digital clock radio under a pile of sketches and watched it, waiting. Something had to happen soon, she told herself.

Five minutes passed, then ten. Fear slunk around the edges of her mind, closing in.

Back to the mirror. She touched the hair, eyebrows, mouth, just to familiarize herself. Well, she already knew what Josh felt like to touch, though from a different viewpoint. Tentatively, she took off the pajama top and stared at Josh's nakedness. Jenny took a deep breath. This was frightening.

"Josh? Are you awake yet?" It was his mother calling him, she realized now.

A response was in order. "Uh, yes. I'll be out in a minute," she said, hoping she sounded enough like Mrs. Friedman's son to allay any suspicions.

What in the world was she thinking of? Of course, Mrs. Friedman would never guess that the Josh she saw was not her true son! If he acted slightly weird, she would just think he was sick or something. She sure wouldn't guess the truth. Nobody would!

Jenny combed Josh's hair. It was wiry, thick, and unruly, unlike her own fine hair. She decided she would just have to change into herself before she had to get dressed to go down to breakfast. This had to be temporary, she told herself nervously. It just had to be. There was no need to worry.

Jenny worried anyway. She shivered, feeling absolutely nauseous. She wondered if Josh was going through the same thing at her house. It was logical, or as logical as this whole crazy thing could be, that they had completely traded places. She wondered what Josh was doing at that very moment.

Fifteen minutes passed. No change whatsoever. Jenny was now frantic to make sense out of this whole thing. She started trembling uncontrollably. What was she to do?

She had to get dressed before Josh's mother came upstairs again. Yet how could she leave this room? Jenny didn't know if she could function in this body. On the way to the closet, she stumbled over Josh's wetsuit and fell against his surfboard, smashing her lip against her top teeth. Often, she'd joked with Josh about drawing up a floor plan, complete with discarded sneakers and clothes in their usual chaos, since he almost never cleaned his room. Now, after fifteen minutes in this mess, she thought he ought to give the idea serious consideration.

She felt awful. She was going to be late for class. She was never late for class. Josh was. Often, he charmed his way into first period, under the intense scowl of Mr. Leviathan, who had exhausted all punishments for tardiness.

Jenny peered into Josh's closet at the neat row of jeans hung on wooden hangers. His shirts were lined up the same way, and she discovered some she'd never seen him wear. And the shoes — all the toes pointed forward, the leather ones polished to a warm, mahogany glow. Jenny had never known he had shoes like that. All she ever saw him wear were the sneakers or cleats that were strewn across his floor. Funny what you learn about a person, poking around in his closet, she thought.

He sure was turning out to be a puzzle, she decided, choosing a pair of jeans and a shirt she knew he liked to wear. The knowledge that she was still trapped in his body felt like a cold piece of lead pressing against her heart. And right now, there was absolutely nothing she could do about it. . . .

She started down to breakfast, very carefully, because she wasn't really sure . . . yes, there it was, Josh's walk. The way he swayed a little when he walked. There was the enchanting little bit of cockiness mixed with boyishness that had first won Jenny over. And that was also the part of Josh that scared her most of all.

No one seemed to notice the slightest difference in Josh when he sauntered into the kitchen and took his usual seat at the table. Thankfully, Jenny remembered where he always sat from eating dinner at the Friedmans'.

"Aren't you making your healthy drink this morning, Josh, dear?" his mother inquired.

Jenny was caught by her blue-eyed stare. Mrs. Friedman was a striking woman, with silvery-blonde hair springing around her face like spun gold. She ran a public relations office. This morning, in her eggshell-white suit, she looked dazzling.

Health drink? Jenny panicked. What did he put in it? Bananas, protein powder, eggs — was that it? A jock's drink to keep Josh in shape.

"Uh, no. I'll just have cornflakes, okay?" Cornflakes were the only visible cereal at the table. Better to ask for those than something they might not have, like her usual, Grapenuts. Generally, Jenny thought that cornflakes tasted like sawdust, but this morning they tasted pretty good.

"Where's Dad?" Jenny asked.

"At work, of course. Don't you realize what time it is?" Mrs. Friedman put down her spoon with a tiny clatter. "He left half an hour ago."

"Oh."

"Are you sick, Josh?" his mother asked with a worried frown.

"Uh, no. I'm fine, Mom." Jenny smiled.

Jenny was amazed she could even *sound* and *act* like Josh — grinning at his mother, getting a kick out of her unfounded worrying.

"Are you ever bright and cheery this morning," Mrs. Friedman commented, looking at the person she believed to be her son. "What got into you?"

Jenny gulped. Quickly, she added, "Oh, I

don't know. I guess it's just that I'm later than usual getting to school, and that makes me really happy. That means a lot less of Mr. Leviathan."

"Do you need a note?"

"Yes, please." Talk about avoiding the whole subject of what-got-into-Josh-Friedman.

"What about after school? Is there baseball practice?" Mrs. Friedman got out a notepad with RACHEL FRIEDMAN printed across the top, and began to write.

Practice after school? A swell of panic blocked Jenny's (or Josh's?) throat. Dance classes took up every day after school, but it was impossible to be in two places at once. Then again, Jenny had no idea if there was baseball practice today.

"Uh, I'm not sure. Might be canceled," she managed. A thick slice of dread lodged in her chest at the idea of playing baseball. Jenny was not particularly athletic, although she was strong.

"There's your excuse for today, but for tomorrow, try getting up earlier." Mrs. Friedman handed her son the note, which was folded in half. "And, by the way, that is the most modest breakfast I've ever seen you eat." She smiled, waiting for a response, but Jenny simply shrugged, not knowing what else to do.

Thankfully, Josh was a good shrugger. Mrs. Friedman turned away.

"Now, leave your dirty clothes outside your

room, so Betsy can wash them. She won't walk into that pigsty of yours. She's afraid of fungus."

"What?"

"She read some article in a health magazine about foot fungi."

"Sounds wild," Jenny said. She went up to Josh's room, picked up his clothes, and piled them dutifully in the hallway. No big deal. Why did he let it get to disaster proportions, Jenny wondered.

Mrs. Friedman called out " 'Bye," and Jenny muttered, "Later," which was a typical response for Josh.

Jenny considered the last few mind-boggling events carefully as she strolled toward the garage. She had planned to drive Josh's Toyota to school, but then remembered that it was in the shop. She would have to walk, which would make her, or him, very late. Waves of panic, like a high sea, splashed over her as she hurried to school.

It seemed that Josh had gotten what he wanted. In a funny, twisted way, his wish had come true.

On the other side of town, Josh Friedman stirred uncomfortably when the alarm went off. In fact, there was something decidedly uncomfortable about the way he felt. It seemed early to him, too early to get up. He was not accustomed to rising before eight A.M., and he wasn't anxious to change that habit.

Josh kept his eyes tightly shut, and covered his ears until the insistent ringing stopped. Then he became aware that the sheets smelled faintly of perfume. Jenny's perfume. Je Reviens. He even liked the sound of the name, and he liked what it meant: "I will return." He imagined Jenny returning to him again and again, wrapped in this aura of great scent.

Those perfume advertisements on TV have nothing on what I think about Jenny, Josh decided as he buried his face in the pillow. And her perfume wasn't even advertised on TV. They always pushed Charlie or Scoundrel, perfumes that were not nearly as nice as Je Reviens. Once, Josh had read that the main ingredient in the best perfumes had the chemical composition of sweat, which was pretty weird. You know darn well you wouldn't walk into a drug store and ask for a bottle of Sweat, and if you named a fragrance that, who would buy it?

Still, what was the reason his sheets smelled of perfume? And what was this disjointed feeling he couldn't shake. The house seemed very busy, and by Josh's internal clock, it was way too early for that much activity. Strange-sounding activity, too. Strange voices. Suddenly he felt an unfamiliar urgency to get up, like his body was actually anxious to get moving.

Open one eye, Josh, he told himself, peeking out from beneath the covers. *Jenny's room*. He felt suddenly, rudely assaulted.

The room swam before his eyes, a blur of pink, white, and yellow. He was dizzy, sick. *What was he doing here? Where was Jenny?* He glanced around in fright, but she was nowhere to be seen.

The room had the feel of Jenny not being present, of her not having been there for awhile. Her clothes hung in a neat row in the open walk-in closet. Sun streamed in through the triangular window, leaving stained glass patterns across the paisley seat fabric, and her books were carefully stacked in one corner of her desk. Jenny was a neat person, that was for sure.

Well, Josh thought, I may as well get up. I mean, what is Jenny's family going to think if they happen to find me in her bed? Total freak out, that's what they'd think. There wouldn't be any words to describe the ensuing drama.

So he pushed back the covers, and faced the biggest shock of his life. Panic shot through him like a series of bullets. If he thought he was sick before, he *knew* he was now. Jenny's body. He was looking down at Jenny's body — *he was in Jenny's shoes!* Sure enough, his, or her, feet fit perfectly into the pink terry slippers by the bedside.

He took a slow inventory, very carefully. Girl arms. Girl legs; long, graceful dancer's legs he'd always admired. And soft, yes, she was soft and velvety, the hair on her arms fine and golden. He looked at her all over with amazement.

He stumbled to the antique dressing table and stared in the mirror at his reflection. Jenny's image stared back at him. He was now Jenny. *No! It couldn't be!*

A scream stuck in his throat. Was this one big joke? No way could he run around being a girl! He had to get out of here! Out of her body! Did the stupid fairy godfather really have anything to do with this? And where was he, anyway?

Naw, he couldn't have, Josh told himself. This was just a large, ridiculous mistake. A dream. Josh slapped Jenny's face and looked in the mirror again. No change. Maybe it was part of some government experiment to switch people around or something. Some new drug. It didn't make any sense at all, he thought, running his fingers over the contours of the face that was not his own.

One thing was for sure — it was awful being somebody else. Just awful. He had never wished for this. He had only wanted Jenny to see what it was like to feel like him, but not *be* him. And he had never, ever, wanted to be in *her* shoes! So when would he wake up from this nightmare?

Josh waited, thinking that time would make the change. He watched the clock tick off the minutes, figuring at least he could keep track of how long it took to change back into his normal self. He wondered how long he'd been this way. Overnight, or just this morning?

Nothing happened for ten minutes. Josh

guessed that if this was real, then Jenny had been transplanted into his body, too. Which was equally weird. And what would she be doing about it? Huh? He kind of wished he'd cleaned up his bedroom, although that would've been out of character. Yet, if he had had a warning of all this, it would have been a nice gesture.

Well, you *did* have a warning, a little voice reminded him, but he shook it away. Yeah, some weird-looking guy calling himself my fairy godfather, speaking out of a computer screen. *That* was a warning? How could you have taken something like that seriously? How could you take *any* of this seriously?

Josh closed his eyes and waited to feel the fuzzy sensation that signals the awakening from a dream. Instead, he heard soft footfalls on the other side of the door.

"Jenny?"

Jenny's mom was calling. She was nice, and always sweet to him.

"Yeah?" he replied as softly as he could.

"Are you up? I didn't hear your radio going, and I thought maybe you'd slept through the alarm."

"No, I'm up. Thanks."

Phew. Close call. He had sounded basically like Jenny then, which was doubly weird. The last time Josh remembered sounding like a girl was when his voice had changed, when he was around twelve. It was the oddest thing, having your voice flip back and forth without your having any control over it. And that's what he felt like now, he decided with an ominous shiver.

Josh was basically a laid-back type of guy. But this really shook him. Shook him down to his toes — which weren't his toes anymore.

Generally, when something upsets you in life, you've always got yourself. But now, Josh didn't even have that. He was Josh-as-Jenny, for three days, if that fairy godfather had been telling the truth. He would be treated like her, unless His Excellency appeared and zipped him out of this body and back into his own. He wondered if there was any way to hurry that process. There was no way of knowing for sure, unless he could summon up the godfather and find out what was going on.

He had to get dressed first. Josh yanked open Jenny's drawers and stared at the folded squares of pastel-colored underwear. He pulled out a bra. *He* was going to wear a *bra*?

Shyly, he put it on, then tried to hook it in the back. When that proved to be difficult, he turned the strap around to the front to secure it, then stared at Jenny's reflection in the mirror. He looked just like a Maidenform ad, he decided.

Then Josh went into Jenny's closet, and scanned the rows of clothes, trying to find something he particularly liked to see Jenny wear. Well, there was this Hawaiian shirt he liked with her white jeans. He looked for the jeans but couldn't find them. So he picked out a pair of light green, stonewashed ones that looked like they might go with the shirt.

This activity kept his mind off the dream he was not awakening from. He was not a fashion-conscious guy, really. He just liked what he saw on Jenny, and she always looked good. Like dressing came naturally to her, and she didn't have to try.

Every few seconds, Josh checked the image in the mirror. Still Jenny, all the way. No visible sign of change. His heart was sinking fast.

Light footsteps made a shuffling sound in the carpeted hallway. Jenny's bedroom door opened.

"Hey, Jenny. Mom wants to know why you haven't unloaded the dishwasher yet." Bernie, Jenny's little brother, reported.

"Tell her I'll be right down," Josh returned, his panic building now, sending sharp needles through his head.

How could he do this? Go to school — as Jenny. A dilemma, with a capital "D."

School. Empty dishwasher. Josh had to get down to the den and try to talk to the fairy godfather before breakfast, even though he was afraid he couldn't function *without* breakfast. Well, he would just have to this morning.

Feeling oddly light, Josh sauntered down the hall into the den, which was at the opposite end of the house. It was a dark, cool room, and he closed the door behind him. If anyone came in asking what Jenny was doing, Josh planned to say he was looking for a computer disk that had some homework on it.

He popped on the diskette he and Jenny had used the day before. He waited. Nothing happened. He popped the diskette out just as he'd done the day before, too, but left the computer turned on.

Then he watched the clock. Five minutes passed. No face. Nothing. Just a blank screen. Where was the guy? He was never real in the first place, Josh told himself. But then how else . . . ?

Right now, I really *need* a fairy godfather, for the first time in my life, and if that vision was really him, then he's not doing me any good, Josh thought ruefully. There was no possible sense to this madness, and now ten minutes had passed and Jenny was due downstairs, to empty the dishwasher and have breakfast.

He decided to give the computer a try later. He was now desperate to get that man on the screen, pin him down, make him break this ridiculous spell or dreamstate, or whatever.

Suddenly, his stomach yawned mightily with hunger. Josh as himself was a regular bottomless pit when it came to food. He had to eat frequent meals, or else he was afraid he would waste away. And he had to have his health drink in the morning. He had no idea what Jenny ate for breakfast, but he sure hoped it was good. He thought about trying to make the health drink in the Knudsons' kitchen. With a fresh stab of fear, he realized he didn't know the first thing about existing in this household.

Reining in his confusion, Josh hurried downstairs and greeted Bernie with a big smile. "Hey, how's it going, Bern?" he asked.

Bernie looked up from his bowl of cereal, and propped his glasses higher on his upturned nose. He knew his sister adored him. He was thirteen, with wheat-blond hair, and a pair of big blue eyes behind the round ovals of his wire-rimmed glasses. He had a studious look, and although he was very smart, he also possessed a large portion of what Josh termed "regular kid." Bernie could play a mean game of Trivial Pursuit, too.

"Fine, Jen." Bernie watched while the person he thought was his sister poked around in the kitchen. "The Grapenuts are on the table. Aren't you having those this morning?"

"I was going to make a health drink."

"Health drink? You?" Bernie got up from the table, squashed an Oakland A's cap down over his blond head, and adjusted its brim.

"Oh, I don't know. Change of pace. I thought it might help with my dancing." Josh located eggs, bananas, milk, honey. There was no protein powder visible in this household, and Josh was pretty sure if he asked for it, the question would be met with confusion. And this was not the time to be under intense scrutiny, even though no one would ever guess the truth. The truth was definitely stranger than fiction.

Josh switched on the blender. The sound

brought Mrs. Knudson into the kitchen.

"What're you doing?" she asked, giving the person she thought was her daughter a light peck on the cheek.

Obviously, using the blender was not part of normal morning procedure. Josh attempted to sound breezy. "Oh, I was just making a health drink. I told Bernie I thought it might help me dance better."

"You're doing marvelously without it, but I guess health food can't harm your success." Mrs. Knudson smiled. She was wearing an Indian print dress with little bells on the neck that tinkled when she bent to put something in her briefcase. She was a university professor, and a real cool one at that, Josh thought. Her hair was the same shade as Jenny's, but cut short, curving gently around her ears. Her expression was generally one of great amusement, the corners of her mouth turned perpetually upward. By contrast, Jenny's face was usually a picture of intense concentration, especially when it came to the subject of dance.

"Well, I'm off, both of you," Mrs. Knudson announced, pecking Bernie on the cheek. "And don't forget the dishwasher, Jenny. You can use the car today — I don't need it. Oh, and by the way, why did you leave your nightgown on the bedroom floor? That's not like you."

"Oh, don't worry, I'll pick it up before *I* leave. See you later, Mom." Josh gulped down the health drink.

After downing two bowls of Grapenuts, which was never one of Josh's favorites, he began work on the dishwasher. Josh had never unloaded a dishwasher before. Betsy, the Friedmans' housekeeper, always did that sort of thing.

Josh unloaded the clean dishes uncertainly and then put everything in the machine — dirty, unrinsed. It looked pretty gross with the variously colored foods all blending together, but he figured if there was enough detergent in the machine, everything would get clean.

Bernie folded clothes on the dining room table. The clothes smelled fresh and warm, and it was on the tip of Josh's tongue to ask why they were doing so much work before school. But he thought better of it. It seemed right, somehow. Jenny always had more chores to do than he did, and of course, so did Bernie. This was a single-parent household; the Knudsons were divorced. No housekeeper. Everyone pitched in. Everyone had a purpose. It was kind of nice.

Then Josh went into Jenny's room to pick up the nightgown and robe that he'd left on the floor. He would have to keep an eye on himself.

As he passed Bernie in the hall, who was delivering piles of clothes to the appropriate rooms, Bernie asked, "Hey, who left the computer on? Was it you?"

"Well, uh, yes, I must have." Panicked (actually, he had not once stopped feeling panicked since awakening), he rushed into the den. He hoped so much to see the fairy godfather staring at him, but no such luck. The jerk had abandoned both him and Jenny, leaving them to fend for themselves. Maybe he would show up later.

Yet a sinking feeling traveled from Josh's (Jenny's?) head, stopped right at stomach-level, and stayed there, like an anchor. The fear that there might be no way out, that both he and Jenny were completely at the mercy of some strange *unknown*, weighed much too heavily. Josh was consumed by fright. He beat his palm against the metal encasement of the computer, too angry and confused to cry.

Then he turned off the computer, checked the clock, and decided it was time for school. *Jenny* time for school, that is. Josh thought of going to school, facing all those people, sitting with Jen's friends instead of his own. Maybe the fairy godfather would make a miraculous appearance. Maybe in his computer science class. He had to. He just had to.

Josh gathered up Jenny's books and strolled out the kitchen door. "See ya, Bernie. Ciao!" he called.

"Yeah, Jen. Have a good one!" Bernie called back.

Climbing into the Knudsons' banged-up VW bug, Josh sorted out his feelings. Or tried to, at least. He was feeling more and more unlike himself.

He seemed particularly conscious of smells.

The odor of gasoline when the car started up, the scent of worn upholstery, the fleeting fragrances of spring flowers as he turned off Bay Street onto Mission Avenue. There was even the salty tang of the ocean on the early morning air.

Josh had always thought himself to be a sensitive type of guy. Sure, he was a jock, but still sensitive. Yet now he was seeing things he had never noticed before, or maybe he was noticing them in a different way.

He was aware of the bright tumble of corn-silk on the stalks in the Community Garden, of how the scarecrow's arm was bent to look like he was beckoning to passersby, of how old Mrs. Hewett's face, as she concentrated on her weeding, was as crinkled as a dried apple.

Was this how Jenny saw things, Josh wondered.

Then he remembered a saying he once heard: Be careful what you wish for, because it may come true. Of course, Josh had never really considered it before. No idle wish of his had ever come true in the past.

As he guided the Knudsons' car through the intersection, Josh decided he would have to start taking life more seriously. But first of all, he had to figure out how to get his body back.

Chapter 3

As the school came into view, Jenny took a deep breath. She had this sudden urge to be invisible for the rest of the day. In an effort to calm herself, she thought: In one hour, I'll turn back into myself. Or, the moment I see Josh, this spell will wear off, right?

Right. Keep hoping, Jenny. She hurried ahead across the school grounds and through the hall without running into anyone. Everyone was in class, where they ought to be. Was this how it was for Josh every morning? Arriving while school was in full swing?

Josh's first period class was American government with Mr. Leviathan, who always gave Josh a bad time about his tardiness. Jenny braced herself and strode into the classroom, hoping she looked every bit as casual as Josh always did.

Mr. Leviathan was writing on the blackboard, but his chalk stopped in mid-scrawl as Jenny entered.

"Well, glad you decided to join us, Mr. Friedman." Mr. Leviathan's smile was not of the really genuine variety, Jenny decided, suppressing a shiver.

"Thank you," she responded, and the class laughed.

"Because we're so pleased to see you this morning, Mr. Friedman, you have become the recipient of a special honor."

Jenny had heard horror stories about this teacher and was not enthusiastic about what he might have up his sleeve.

"Oh, yeah?" she said lightly, hoping she sounded like Josh.

"*Yeah*," Mr. Leviathan mimicked, then licked his lips with obvious delight. "The recital of the preamble of the Constitution has been saved for you. Now if you will take your place in front of my desk here, and begin."

The teacher stepped aside, positioning himself next to the American flag in the corner, which rocked a little on its spindly pedestal. The class snickered.

The roomful of expectant faces shimmered before her. Jenny swallowed her fear and began reciting. "We, the people of the United States, in order to form a more perfect union. . . ."

When she was finished, the class clapped.

"Hey, pretty good, Friedman," Terry Fields called out.

"Way to go," one of the other boys added.

Jenny smiled and glanced at Mr. Leviathan, who could only manage a scowl.

"I suppose that as with everything in life, practice makes perfect, Mr. Friedman," he said coolly. "It is a pity that you can't seem to apply that concept to punctuality as easily as you do to memorization."

Jenny was a little frightened. "Are they alike?" she asked with utmost seriousness and sincerity. The class laughed.

Mr. Leviathan snorted, muttered under his breath, and ordered Josh to take his seat.

Jenny sat down. She had trouble concentrating on the lecture, which was about state governments. Besides, being Josh meant being a little physically uncomfortable at a small school desk, a problem she'd never considered before.

Finally, the bell rang. Everyone sprang from their seats while Mr. Leviathan shouted out last minute assignment orders. Jenny scooped up her books, and awkwardly squeezed herself out of the desk chair.

Terry Fields, one of Josh's good friends, fell in step beside Jenny as she was leaving.

"Hey, Josh, you did a great job." He slapped her on the back.

"Uh, thanks." Jenny recoiled in surprise at the force of the slap. She realized it was meant to be friendly. That was just the way guys were — physical.

"You sure you didn't have the words written on the back of your hand?" Terry teased.

His grin revealed a chipped tooth, and his baseball cap was tilted sideways over tight brown curls.

"Not this time, Terry," Jenny said. She wanted to ask about baseball practice, but it would look strange, and besides, she would probably be turned back into herself by the time school was over, anyway.

"We've got track in gym today," Terry pointed out as they walked down the hall.

"Oh, yeah, right." Jenny shivered, realizing that the next period was PE. Which meant she would be a girl in a boys' gym. Ordinarily, that was the kind of thing a girl might wonder about, but know it was never going to happen. Not unless you were forcibly shoved into the boys' gym door by a group of giggling friends, or you couldn't read English and wandered in there by accident.

Oh, please, Josh, where are you, she pleaded silently, as she and Terry strode into the boys' locker room.

She followed Terry around the first row of lockers, concentrating on his back. When Terry stopped in front of his locker, Jenny bumped into him.

"What're you doing, Friedman? Your locker's over there." He motioned in the direction of the next row. "You share with Ryan, remember?"

"Right." Jenny wandered toward the lockers, looking for Rob Ryan, a squarely built boy who was sitting on the bench that ran between lockers — in his jockey shorts!

"How goes it, Friedman?" Rob grinned, pulling on one soiled sports sock, which reached the bottom of his hairy knee.

"Uh, hi," Jenny gulped, and scanned the lockers. Anything to keep her eyes off Rob. Why didn't he hurry up and get dressed? She was naturally curious and all that, but somehow, this situation was a little too unnerving.

Thankfully, Josh's locker was open — she recognized the unraveled name tag on his gray T-shirt. She pulled the T-shirt out, and with it came a pair of socks and shorts.

Uh-oh. Next step — change into your gym clothes in front of all these guys. A fresh wave of realization broke over Jenny — not to worry, she had a guy's body. No one would ever know she was an imposter.

Slowly, she pulled off Josh's clothes. Her fingers fumbled with the unfamiliar garments. In her nervousness, she folded them carefully and laid them on the bench. Then she slid into the wrinkled shorts and T-shirt. She wondered when was the last time Josh had taken his clothes home to wash them.

"Friedman, what's gotten into you? You never fold your clothes, man," Rob remarked in pure horror, almost disgust.

"Yeah, well, I'm on a new program. This is the new me."

"Sure, man. You're a born-again neat person, I know." Rob cackled, pulling on his shorts. Then he zipped his sweatshirt.

Boys in various stages of undress passed

before Jenny. Here were guys she saw every day in school, now walking around in jockey shorts and socks. At this point it wasn't much different than seeing them in bathing suits at the beach, but still. . . .

She hurried outside, where Coach Jacobs eyeballed Josh's gym clothes critically in the line up next to the track. "Hey, Friedman, it might be a good idea to get those clothes within throwing distance of a washing machine," he bellowed snidely.

"This weekend," Jenny promised, certain that would be Josh's response. The coach was a gruffer version of her dance instructor, Mrs. Herbert.

Thankfully, the coach turned his attention to the other students. Jenny looked down at the oversized jogging shoes, wondering how she was going to keep up with the rest of the class. Running was not her thing. Sure, she was limber and active, but Josh was a *real* runner. Now dance. . . . If she could dance along the track. . . . But in this body?

Ugh. The coach ordered everyone down for situps and pushups, fifty of each. Situps were fine; Jenny did enough of those in her regular workout to be able to keep up with the rest, but boys' pushups were a different story. In Josh's body, however, she was able to do them pretty easily. For a moment, she even enjoyed the feeling of breezing through an activity which had been so hard for her in her own body.

Across the field, the girls' gym class was in session, doing aerobics. Jenny wondered how Josh was doing. Was he making a laughingstock of himself? And what about later, if he had to go to her dance class? How would he manage that?

Maybe by that time the fairy godfather will have us back in our own bodies, she told herself hopefully. This is ridiculous. She wanted to see Josh so much, to know that he was all right, just to know he still existed.

Jenny watched Tabitha Ballinger lead the rest of the girls out to the baseball diamond. Her long black hair was pulled into a ponytail which swung as she ran, and a few of the boys turned to watch her.

"Nice bod," Freddie Halbrecht remarked, grinning at the other boys.

"Yeah. Gonna ask her out, Fred?" Gary Krupp asked him.

"Been thinking about it," Freddie's eyes followed Tabitha from home plate to first base as she made her first hit.

"She might not go out with you," Gary teased. "I hear she's uptight — only dates computer nerds."

"Oh, can it, will ya, Krupp? She'll go out with me. Who could resist?" Freddie raised one eyebrow in what he thought was a sexy expression.

Jenny groaned inwardly. Freddie with his tousled, surf-blond hair and tanned good looks probably wouldn't have any trouble, but he could leave his ego and personality at home, as far as she was concerned. He was a conceited pain.

"There's Rhonda. She'll go out with you, for sure," Gary suggested, pointing out the thin girl up at bat.

Freddie scoffed at that idea. "She'll go out with anybody. Is there anybody at this high school she hasn't dated?"

"I don't think that's fair!" exclaimed Jenny hotly. "I happen to know Rhonda is a very nice person!"

The guys all stared at Josh as though he was from Mars.

"Well, yeah, we know you're a softie, Friedman," Freddie said. "We were just having fun."

"What if she were to say things like that about you?"

"It would all be true!" Freddie said, and the others burst into appreciative laughter.

Jenny felt like an alien, but she didn't care. She was angry with all of them. She knew Rhonda had a reputation, but she didn't like hearing the boys talk about her this way. How awful to be the subject of such cruel discussion! And how could they be so mean?

"Hey, Josh, what're ya dreaming about?" shouted the coach. "Get out there on the track, please. We've got a four-forty to run here."

"He said 'please.' Coach never says 'please,'" noted Freddie gleefully.

Jenny took Josh's place, crouching down with her fingers in the gravel of the track next to Gary. There were five other boys besides the two of them. Jenny took a deep breath.

"Josh'll beat them, no trouble," she heard someone mutter behind them. A shiver ran through her in response to that expectation.

"On your mark, get set, GO!" shouted the coach, pressing the button down on his stopwatch.

Jenny felt herself as Josh, launching with full force, legs pumping rhythmically beneath her, heart pounding in her ears. Exhilarating, that's what it was. Exhilarating being Josh. Like dancing, only in a different way. She was carried along by this foreign being thudding along the track. Gary came along next to her. She pushed harder. Gary passed the guy he thought was Josh, his lips parting in a smile. Jenny decided to just pace herself, to run evenly, but without great speed, until close to the end of the laps. She'd heard Josh talk about track enough times to know that was what he did.

Josh Friedman's time was mediocre. A surprise to his coach, and to most of the other guys.

"I think that's the slowest on record for you, Josh," remarked the coach, slapping Josh's back. Jenny cringed. "I've never seen you fall so far behind."

"Maybe we'll be able to beat you yet, Friedman," Tommy Southern said hopefully.

"Not if I can help it." Jenny responded like Josh would.

"Race ya?" Tommy challenged, lining up next to Jenny. Wearily, she raced him to the gym.

As they neared the gym, the roar of the showers met Jenny's ears. Steam billowed around the naked male bodies.

There was Rob, scrubbing his hair and rinsing it under the hot water. Soap streaked down his chest. Jenny couldn't stop staring. There was Sean Cunningham cupping his hand around the jet stream of water to shoot it into Eddie Collander's eyes. Their laughter reverberated off the tiled walls. She closed her eyes.

"Friedman, quit your daydreaming, will ya? No wonder you did lousy today." Rob regarded his friend critically. "You sure you're not on something?"

Jenny stood stock-still, while waves of panic crashed over her. "No, just your basic space case," she murmured. If he only knew, she thought, filled with the knowledge that she had to get undressed and shower with the boys.

A couple of guys ran past, towel-whipping each other. Their activity was noisy, aggressive, markedly unfamiliar.

Tentatively, Jenny took off Josh's dirty gym clothes. Act natural, she thought. Just wash and get some clothes on, fast.

But she *couldn't* take a shower with them.

Terrified, she pulled on Josh's jeans and quickly buttoned his shirt. Then she took his dirty gym clothes and stuffed them in his sports bag to take home for washing.

One of the guys glanced up. "Hey, Friedman, what're you doing? Aren't you gonna shower?"

"Hey, Friedman, you dirty slob!" another called.

"I'm not sitting next to you next period!"

"Oink! Oink!"

The taunts followed Jenny as she fled from the gym. She wanted to cry, but did her best not to. Along with the tears came the realization that boys didn't run off crying. Josh would be teased unmercifully for being some kind of a sissy. Jenny could see that being a boy carried with it the difficult responsibility of acting the way people thought a boy should act.

Chapter 4

Josh hurried across the front lawn of the school, trying to remember what Jenny had first period. Music history. That's right. And what were they studying?

He *had* to find Jenny. This was just too much. He didn't know her locker combination so he couldn't get her books out. He wouldn't know any of her assignments. And he didn't like being early.

Josh was so absorbed in his thoughts that he plowed right into Jenny's best friend, Elyse Roberts.

The short, dark-haired girl bounced back in surprise. "Jenny? Where are you going? You didn't even see me!" she cried.

"Oh, sorry, Elyse. I was so deep in thought I wasn't paying attention."

"Well, you'd better come back to earth. You could get hurt walking around like that." Elyse had this caring way about her that Josh hadn't really noticed before.

Her dark brown eyes focused on the stonewashed jeans Josh was wearing. "Hey, I've never seen you wear those jeans with that shirt. Looks . . . interesting."

"You don't sound too sure."

"Well, it takes a little getting used to. Purple Hawaiian shirt and green jeans, you know."

Josh walked into the building next to Elyse, and stopped with her to talk to a group of Jenny and Elyse's friends. He hoped he looked okay. He hadn't expected Elyse to notice Jenny's clothes.

"Hi, Jenny. How're ya doing?" Connie Bevelman, a petite blonde girl, asked.

"Just fine, and you?" Josh responded nervously.

"Great. My mom and I had this big heart-to-heart talk this morning and we got everything all figured out." Connie beamed.

"Did I miss something?" Josh blinked.

"About how upset I've been that she's marrying Frankfurter. You know." She sounded exasperated. Jenny should know.

"Oh, yeah, right. Why do you call him Frankfurter, I forgot?" Josh asked, trying to get information.

"His name is Frank, that's the only reason. Well, you know how mad I've been about this and my mom taking the new job and never being home," Connie said impatiently.

"Uh-huh."

"I just feel so much better. I wonder why I waited so long to talk about these things, don't you?" Connie continued.

"No, I mean yes," Josh cried.

Josh couldn't remember the last time he and his mom had had a heart-to-heart talk. She was always worrying about him getting into trouble, and took that crazy class about understanding teenagers, but they never actually talked about specific problems.

"My parents and I don't communicate at all." Toni Wiseman sighed, slamming her locker door shut. "It's just 'Pass the sugar' with us."

"My father only talks to me at report card time," someone else said.

They all laughed as the first bell rang.

Elyse glanced at her Swatch watch. "Hey, I've gotta run. See ya at lunch — 'Bye," she called as she ran off.

Which meant Josh had to move, too. He climbed the stairs to music history. Ms. Mumper was the teacher. Josh had never had her before, but he figured that if Jenny liked her, she must be okay.

The teacher was about fifty, heavyset, with a sharp-featured face. She wore a patchwork skirt and a long shirt belted at the waist. Her hair was kind of stringy and long, and she looked like an aging hippie to many students, Josh included.

One of Jenny's friends, Cathy Bowen, sat in a corner seat. She looked like she'd been crying.

"What's wrong?" Josh asked impulsively.

"Oh, Jenny. Doug and I are breaking up," Cathy sniffled. "He wants to date other people. He says we're getting too serious. I feel so awful, I just want to die!"

Josh was baffled. She wanted to die . . . over Doug Kalinsky? That klutz who couldn't even pitch straight?

"Hey, I'm sure it's not as bad as all that," Josh said sympathetically.

"It's worse. We'll never see each other again. Or we wouldn't see each other ever if we didn't have to go to the same school." She buried her face in a handkerchief. There was a little Dutch boy appliquéd in one corner of it.

"This isn't the end of the world, I'm sure," Josh offered.

"Yes, it is, it definitely is." She gave a shaky sigh. "I mean, now I have to watch him flirting with other girls. I can't stop thinking about him. I have to see him around school, and I won't be able to *bear* it if he starts to date someone else!"

Cathy was working her way up to full-fledged hysteria, in Josh's opinion. He was uncomfortable, so he changed the subject.

"What're we studying in this class, anyway?" he asked casually, looking over Cathy's shoulder at the textbook on her desk. He didn't know how to react to her outburst. When Jenny cried over something, he just stood there, not quite sure of what to do with himself.

"Oh, Vivaldi. Why don't you know that? You're Ms. Musical, aren't you?" Cathy frowned through her tears. She looked annoyed at Jenny, but Josh couldn't understand why.

"Oh, uh, yeah, but I forgot about Vivaldi. I've got an audition coming up and I'm nervous." Josh exhaled through his teeth. He wished Jenny had left part of her brain behind so that he could consult her on what was going in this class, and with Cathy. Music history and girls' emotions were crazy stuff.

The bell rang. Cathy wiped her eyes and turned around in her seat. Josh also faced forward, hoping that Jenny wouldn't be called upon for anything.

As Ms. Mumper read the morning bulletin, he let his mind rove forward over the day, figuring that the next thing he'd better do after this class was to find Jenny. Maybe if they saw each other, Josh hoped, this whole mess would straighten itself out.

"Jenny Knudson," Ms. Mumper's voice resounded with exasperation. "Are you there, my dear?"

The teacher flourished her pen in the air as though trying to elicit Jenny's response by movement. Josh realized she was focusing on him and jumped to attention.

"Uh, yes. I'm sorry. I have a lot on my mind," he muttered, feeling Jenny's cheeks heat up.

"You should have. I've called your name twice already and you are still out to breakfast," Ms. Mumper huffed, and the class laughed. She cleared her throat. "The question I pose to you is this: In what year was Antonio Vivaldi born?"

Better to give a wrong answer than an I-don't-know, Josh figured. And he sure didn't know the answer to that one. Sweat broke out across Jenny's forehead.

But then an amazing thing happened. Cathy leaned her chin in her hand, which shifted her slightly in her seat and gave Josh a view of her open textbook. There was a picture of a composer with a caption under it, which read "Antonio Vivaldi, 1675?–1741."

Josh faced Ms. Mumper triumphantly. "Well, they think Vivaldi was born in 1675, but there's a question mark after that date."

"Why do you think that is, Jenny?" Ms. Mumper questioned.

Josh shrugged. "Maybe he didn't want anyone to know his true age."

The class laughed.

"You are rather mischievous this morning, Ms. Knudson," Ms. Mumper's lips turned upward in a smile. He guessed this was pretty out-of-line behavior for Jenny, and probably good old Vivaldi was no joking matter.

Fortunately, Ms. Mumper turned to another student, Ronnie Gray, and asked him what he thought. Josh didn't listen for the answer. He waited for the bell to ring so that he could find Jenny, and himself — in the true sense of the phrase.

* * *

A strange sensation overtook Josh as he glimpsed Jenny standing at his locker. How often does a person get to look at himself doing something perfectly normal, but from a distance? Maybe you can see yourself paying for an album on the closed circuit TV in the record store, Josh thought, but that's not the same thing. This was no TV image, it was reality, and it almost knocked Josh over. He ran down the hall, marveling at the lightness of Jenny's body as he skipped through the crowd.

"Jenny."

Automatically, Jenny in Josh's body turned around. She smiled at him, or actually, at herself.

"I meant Josh," he whispered, kissing her with relief. Then he said, "I've never kissed myself before."

"Oh, Josh, I've been looking all over for you!" Jenny cried. "What're we going to do?"

"I don't know," he said, keeping his voice low. "Geez, it really happened! I couldn't quite believe it until I saw you."

"Yeah, I thought the same thing. But I was hoping maybe seeing you would make us change back, you know? He can't mean it — leaving us this way!"

"He said three days, Jenny. We can't be stuck this way for that long. I tried your computer this morning, like we did yesterday, but nothing happened. *No communicado.* The guy's vanished."

"My dress rehearsal on Saturday! I have to practice! We've got to find that fairy godfather and demand our bodies back," Jenny declared.

"Absolutely. We'll get on it right away. Apprehend the perpetrator," he said, feeling a need to hear something funny in the face of this disaster.

"Josh, stop with the jokes!" Jenny stifled a laugh.

People turned around to look at them. "Can't you just see us filing a formal complaint about our personal out-of-body experiences? We'd get two one-way tickets to an asylum," Josh moaned.

"I suppose we could try the *National Enquirer*," Jenny suggested.

Josh shrugged, and looked at himself critically. "Hey, I like what you're wearing."

"Thanks. I'm not so sure I would wear those pants with that shirt, though." She eyed his choice of her clothes critically.

"Elyse mentioned it, too. Oh, well, better luck next time." They moved away from the lockers.

"You saw Elyse?" Jenny asked.

"You sound so funny as me," Josh said.

"Yeah, well likewise."

"I ran into her on the way into school. Literally. I was spaced out," Josh said.

Jenny groaned. "To be expected."

"Let's get some lunch," Josh suggested. "You're starved."

They both laughed. Being together and

laughing melted the cold fear inside them for the moment.

In the cafeteria Josh grabbed a couple of trays and handed one to Jenny, just like he always did.

They sat down together and distributed the food. It was their regular routine, only switched around. Jenny sipped at her milk, looking longingly at Josh's diet plate. Josh wished he could devour Jenny's roast beef sandwich and French fries.

Josh started talking. "I have, I mean, *you* have computer sicence next period. Why don't we get into the room before the class and see if we can find the fairy godfather–"

"Fine. And what if the teacher sees him?"

"That would be great," Josh exclaimed. "Mr. Leipzig could be a witness in our behalf. This could be the beginning of a long and profitable career for us."

Jenny blinked. "As freaks?"

They finished their lunch quickly and left for the computer science room. The door was unlocked, so Jenny and Josh slipped in and turned on the lights.

Jenny sat down in front of one of the monitors, and switched the computer on. She put in a game diskette, then waited. The light from the screen cast a green glow over her fingers on the keyboard.

"Where are you, Godfather?" Josh asked, punching the keys over Jenny's, or his, shoulder. Then he pointed at the screen,

Uncle Sam–style. "We want *you*!" he ordered.

"We wish you were here!" Jenny added. Including the word *wish* seemed like a good idea.

But he didn't show, and the bell rang. Josh leaned back against the seat, speaking in a robot monotone. "We have now entered the *Twilight Zone*. We are now seeking a weird little man in a computer. It does not compute."

Just then Mr. Leipzig entered. *"What* doesn't compute?" the teacher asked Josh with amusement.

"Oh, uh, nothing. There's an explanation for everything — I think," Jenny spoke up. Now any attempt to bring up the face was lost with the teacher in the room, especially with him peering over Josh's shoulder.

Josh turned to Jenny. "I just remembered. I left my book in the cafeteria. Will you come with me to get it?"

"Sure." Jenny was relieved to have an excuse to get away from Mr. Leipzig's scrutiny.

The teacher looked from one to the other as they got up and left the classroom. Outside, Josh ripped a piece of paper out of his notebook. "Tell me your schedule, and as much info as you can about your classes. I think we're going to be stuck this way all afternoon."

Jenny outlined the afternoon for Josh. He did the same for her.

"Meet me at your locker after school, okay?" Josh asked.

"Okay," Jenny promised.

"Hey," Josh cupped her face in his hands (boy, was that confusing). "One thing we can be thankful for."

"What's that?" Jenny looked doubtful.

"He didn't say it would be forever." Josh smiled.

"I'll count my blessings, Josh."

Chapter 5

After school, Jenny and Josh met at her locker. He got out what she needed and they started down the hall.

"Hey, aren't you going to carry my books for me?" Josh asked her.

"Oh, uh, sure. I forgot my manners." Jenny took the load of books. "Oh, Josh, this is so *strange!* Me carrying your books, I mean . . . there's such a thing as role reversal, but. . . ."

Jenny paused, then asked, "So what do we do now?"

"Go to your house and see if we can't make contact." Josh motioned to the side door of the school building. "My car's parked out here."

"You mean *my* car."

"Oh, right. Well, possession is nine tenths of the law," he joked, leading the way across the parking lot.

"Does that apply to bodies as well?" Jenny

questioned, watching an impish expression cross her own features.

"It must. I've been after possession of yours for long enough."

"Is that all you ever think of?" Jenny teased.

"Of course not!" he countered.

They climbed into Jenny's car. Jenny thought how uncomfortable the small car was in Josh's body. It was the perfect size for her, when she was herself.

"Well, sometimes I wonder if you have a one-track mind, especially after what I went through today." Then Jenny related her experience in the boys' gym class.

Josh laughed. "If only the guys knew!"

"I got so freaked out, I left without taking a shower."

"Oh, no, really? Those guys'll be ribbing me for a long time. How about track? How'd I do?"

"Not well. Everybody was teasing you about your slow time." Jenny sat back in her seat and added, "And the guys were making mean remarks about Rhonda Nygard. They were so obnoxious!"

Josh shrugged. "Oh, they always do that."

Jenny decided to change the subject. "I'm worried. If we don't get our bodies back — I know this isn't a pleasant thought — but how are you going to dance for me this afternoon?"

An arrow of fear pierced Jenny as she envisioned Josh at her class. What would happen there? Surely, he wouldn't be able to do that complicated routine, which she had been working on for months. And to think her ballet career depended upon it. This switch couldn't have happened at a worse time.

"Hey, Jen," Josh held up a fist. "You're talking to a champion gymnast here. I can do anything!"

"Uh-huh. You *do* realize what this rehearsal is all about for me this weekend?" she asked, turning to look at him.

"I think I've only heard that a thousand times, but I never thought it would apply directly to me," he told her. "Have you no confidence in me?"

"It's not a matter of confidence," she said. Then just what was it a matter of, she wondered.

"How about baseball practice?" Josh countered. "Will you do all right?"

She took a deep breath. "Look, this is ridiculous. By then, I'm sure we'll be ourselves. This can only go on so long, right? I miss being myself."

"Yeah, me, too. I never realized how attached I was to myself until I became you. And I'm starting to realize just how weird girls are. Like this morning, Cathy Bowen was crying because she and Doug are breaking up," Josh complained.

"Oh, no! That's awful! She must be broken-hearted," Jenny frowned in concern. "I've got to see her."

"You *can't* see her, Jenny. You're not yourself," Josh was quick to remind her. "She wouldn't talk to you."

"So what did you say? Did you comfort her?" Jenny asked.

He shrugged. "I don't know. I said something like 'It's not the end of the world.' But she was really broken up about it."

"Of course she was broken up about it! Wouldn't you be upset if it happened to us?"

"Well, sure." Hesitantly, Josh asked, "Hey, Jen, *we're* okay, aren't we?"

She giggled. "Well, right now, we aren't even *normal*. But we'd better stick together, because the only person who understands what you're going through right now is me, and vice versa."

There was a small measure of comfort in that.

"And now I have to tell you about dance class." Jenny was eager to change the subject. "My leotard is in my top right-hand dresser drawer, where I put it the other day."

"Yesterday," Josh corrected her.

That word startled Jenny. *Yesterday*. Back when they were normal.

"Yes, yesterday. The teacher's name is Mrs. Herbert, and she's expecting me to know this dance. I'll go through it once for you when we get to my house."

"This is the dance that's taken you months to get straight?" Josh cried.

"Yes, I'm afraid so."

"Man, I'm dead meat."

Jenny sighed. "That is not a comfortable thought. Considering whose skin you're walking around in."

Fortunately, no one else was home when they got to Jenny's house. The first thing Josh and Jenny did was to go into the den and try to bring the fairy godfather on the computer screen.

Josh stared at the computer, muttering under his breath. "Come on, you stranger. Come out of there and tell us what to do!"

"He sure is being stubborn, Josh." Jenny peered at the blank screen.

"He's not very obedient," Josh complained. "I mean, what nerve he has to go around granting wishes and then leaving people to fend for themselves," Josh declared. "Someone could get hurt."

Jenny's spirits took a nose dive as she stared at the screen. She glanced at Josh as herself. "Maybe he's not available at the moment," she suggested.

"He must be on an emergency house call," he returned. "Let's give him a chance to get back to the office."

Josh reset the machine and called up the game diskette again, but there was no sign of the man.

"Some fairy godfather. He's unreliable, Jen."

Jenny got up and paced around the room. "At least we know what to expect. Three days, whether we like it or not."

"Yeah." Josh sighed heavily. "I guess we've got no choice. Come on. Let's see how I do as a dancer."

In the den, Jenny put a Chopin album on the stereo, then clumsily attempted the dance for Josh. She was dancing a solo in the overture, and two dances from *Les Sylphides*, a romantic ballet.

Josh laughed, watching his own body leaping around the den.

"Stop laughing," Jenny ordered. "You don't know how hard this is. I feel like a baby elephant."

"I'm ready with the trunk jokes," he said, then caught her glare. "No, seriously, I'm sure it's very hard. I can't imagine doing that." Josh supressed a smirk.

"Well, you'd *better* start imagining. You're the champion gymnast, after all." Jenny flounced through the next segment, quickly reaching the exasperation point.

"Uh-huh. Okay." He got up and tried a few steps.

"No, no, this way. Your timing's way off!" said Jenny, exasperated.

"Well, your demo leaves a lot to be desired," Josh said. "I don't think either of us is up to a major performance at this time."

"It's not funny," Jenny blurted out, feeling close to tears. Everything she'd worked so hard for seemed threatened now.

"Look, Jen, if you're going to be me, you can't get all emotional about this. You're a guy. You're tough, remember?"

"Yeah, a real macho man. I eat nails for breakfast." She flexed Josh's muscles.

"Jenny, this no joke. Serious stuff. Guys are in control at all times."

"Why is it only serious when we're talking about *you*? Don't you think my emotions are important?" Jenny cried.

"Not at this point, to be honest," he answered.

"I get the feeling you don't take me very seriously, Josh." Jenny now stood with hands on hips, glaring at him.

"C'mon, Jenny, let's not argue. I take you real seriously, see?" He made a face, supposedly full of concern. "Now let's go out to the backyard and see how you hit a baseball."

How Jenny hit a baseball, even in Josh's experienced body, was nothing to get excited about. She'd played ball in the street as a little kid, but that was a long time ago.

Josh stood in the center of the yard, pitching balls that Jenny swung at repeatedly and missed. "Choke up on that bat, Jen. Come on, you can do it."

She did as he said.

"Keep your eye on that ball. Don't swing yet, wait till it gets to you. That's right. Aw, darn!"

Jenny was slightly awed by the sight of herself pitching so well, and also found it very disconcerting trying to hit the ball. Besides, Josh's arms and hands were big in comparison with her own — she felt like she had paws. Swinging at the ball sent her slightly off balance.

Finally, after several futile attempts, Jenny said, "Josh, you've got to go. I have a dance class and you've got to be there."

He walked over and handed her the ball. "Oh, all right. But I'd much rather play ball." They kissed briefly, still unused to the idea of kissing each other this way. "I'll give you a ride to my house."

At Josh's house, they kissed each other again, and Jenny went up the flagstone walk to the front door. Fortunately, the only person around was the housekeeper, Betsy. Jenny went straight to Josh's room and looked around for his baseball uniform. Of course, she tripped over his cleats. They weren't hard to find, only hard to avoid killing yourself on.

Checking the bedside clock, Jenny quickly dressed in the uniform, and snuck out while the housekeeper vacuumed the opposite end of the hallway.

"Friedman, you're in trouble, d'you know that?" Coach Jacobs yelled, his face screwed up into a mass of wrinkles.

Jenny tensed at this verbal attack. She'd forgotten she had to see the obnoxious coach for baseball as well as PE. Oh, well, it was only for three days.

Josh's team was called the Druids. For the sake of practice, the team divided itself in half in order to play a practice game.

Jenny was positioned at first base. Nervously, she punched Josh's glove, having just missed a ball thrown by Willie Edwards, the pitcher. Willie wagged his head in disgust.

Jenny felt like a klutz. She did not feel in control, as Josh assured her guys were supposed to be. Sorry, Josh, she mentally apologized. She got ready for the next play. Eddie Collander was up to bat, hunched over the plate like a big question mark.

The crack of bat hitting ball resounded across the field. The ball soared above the outfielders, who ran with their eyes following it, their mitts outstretched. Sean Cunningham caught and dropped the ball. Eddie ran like a rabbit and made a home run, bringing base runners Walt Collins and Benjamin Stein in with him. Eddie's team leaped up and down in ecstasy.

That made the score three to zero. Two outs. The pitcher threw the ball to Doug Kalinsky, who hit a fly. Willie caught it.

In the dugout, the coach came over to Jenny. "I sure hope you hit better than you catch today, Friedman. I can't figure you out. What're we gonna do with you?"

Jenny felt like shriveling inside this strange skin. "I don't know. I might have a touch of the flu," she said.

" 'A touch of the flu'?" the coach mimicked her words. "Yeah, well maybe you do act sick, but I'm losing patience. Maybe you need to go home and sleep it off, whatever it is." The coached scratched his bald head. "I've had no-shows and I've heard every excuse in the book, but I've never had a player with such a drastic shift in performance.

"I'm sorry. I'm sure I'll be better by Friday's game." she tried to appease him, feeling absolutely awful. Performance. She knew what that was all about. Oh, Josh, I'm so sorry, she thought.

She sat watching the others bat. Gary Krupp made a home run, Cecil Morris walked to base, and Terry Fields struck out.

"Your turn, Friedman," Coach Jacobs said. "And please, make it good this time. You're lucky this is just practice."

Jenny breathed deeply. She selected a bat, a good, thick wooden one, much like the one she and Josh had played with in the backyard. She sauntered over to the plate, and hunched over it as she'd seen the others do.

Freddie Halbrecht pitched fast, clean, and right over the plate.

"Strike one!" called the umpire.

Freddie pitched again. This time Jenny choked up on the bat, like Josh had told her to. Mentally, she timed it, and swung.

"Strike two!"

"Come on, Friedman!" growled the coach from behind.

Jenny shivered, planting Josh's feet more firmly in the dirt, being careful not to look the slightest bit girlish.

The next pitch came fast and hard. When Jenny swung, she nearly fell over.

"Strike three! You're out!"

The harsh words rang in the air, throbbing around Jenny.

"Next up!"

The coach came over and leaned his hand on Josh's shoulder. "Get some sleep. Have your mother make you some chicken soup. Get well, kid. We've got a game coming up."

Finally, practice came to an end. Jenny grabbed an armful of bats and shoved them in the soiled equipment bag, feeling tired. She couldn't wait to get home, or to Josh's home, and just lie down.

In fact, thinking from the inside out, always thinking, of how and what to do next, was exhausting. After only one day in Josh's body, she felt as though she was in a foreign country and couldn't speak the language.

And it wasn't just his regular language, it was the language boys used that baffled Jenny the most. Like they didn't care about how anyone felt. She understood pushing yourself physically to your utmost limits, but keeping up an image of strength the way boys thought you should was something new to her. How long had they been like that, Jenny wondered.

Being a boy was definitely different. The strain of being Josh stretched her taut like a rubber band, not letting her relax for a minute. Three days of this was liable to drive her crazy.

She wondered if Josh felt the same way about being her.

Chapter 6

Josh stood at the ballet barre, concentrating as hard as he could on the back of the dancer in front of him. He watched every movement the girl made carefully, and every once in a while would check in the mirror to see how Jenny was doing.

They were doing *pliés*, bending their knees while keeping their backs straight. No sweat, he thought at first. But quickly he realized that it looked easy, but it had to be done as if you were balancing a pile of books on your head.

"Jenny Knudson! What do you think you're doing?" asked Mrs. Herbert, a petite, muscular woman whose straight-backed self-confidence filled the studio as she marched over to her student.

Josh shivered in Jenny's toe shoes, which felt pretty strange. Fortunately, Jenny's toes were pretty tough and used to this weird treatment. Josh was limber from exercise, but even so, he wasn't able to do the things

Jenny had coached him on before this class. Impossible.

"Jenny, I can't believe this is you today." Mrs. Herbert's voice rose with incredulity. "You are not the same student! Are you sure you're all right?"

"Well, I have been feeling kind of out of it lately," Josh admitted.

Mrs. Herbert's eyes narrowed, her mouth pursed with worry. "I'm sorry to hear that Jennifer. You are certainly not yourself. We must define what is wrong, and get you sorted out." She lowered her voice conspiratorially. "You're our greatest hope for the summer school, you know."

"I get your drift." Josh nodded and smiled. Mrs. Herbert blinked in surprise, but let the comment go. Josh realized the teacher wasn't used to hearing Jenny talk that way. Oh, well, more was different about this Jenny than met the eye.

Mrs. Herbert waved her thin, twiglike fingers in the air. "All right, class. Now, *plié*, here we go! One-two-three-and-four and one-two-three-and-four, and. . . ."

Josh *pliéd*, eliciting a dark scowl from Mrs. Herbert, who waved him on impatiently. He finished the exercise sloppily, wishing like crazy Jenny could just zip right into her own body and straighten this mess out.

She had warned him that warm-ups at the barre were harder than they looked. He'd even watched her doing them. She was beautiful at it, so graceful.

Going to school in Jen's body was one thing, but dancing was definitely another. Sure, he knew there were boy ballet dancers, but he had never dreamed of being one. It seemed like such a feminine thing to be. He wasn't one of those guys who would make fun of a guy who wanted to be one, but it wasn't for him.

Briefly, he wondered what Jenny was doing in *his* place. He had become worried when she'd said he did badly in track. Of course, he could fix that when he was back in his own body, but he hated to give the guys anything to razz him about.

He looked up to find Mrs. Herbert wagging her head at him in exasperation. "You're making a rotary motion with that leg, Jennifer," she reminded her pupil. He supposed that was bad.

Josh followed the example of the other students as best he could, and then it was time to leave the barre and practice the dance itself.

The class was doing three dances from *Les Sylphides* for the summer school auditions. The characters were sylphs, or fairy-like people of the air. Jenny had made it sound and look so beautiful when she had shown it to him once, so Josh knew basically what it was supposed to be like, and plunged in.

"Stop! Stop! Stop!" Mrs. Herbert demanded, holding up her hand.

Josh stopped. In the mirror, Jenny looked

like a stork balanced at an ungainly angle —
not at all like the graceful ballerina she was.

Behind Josh, a group of students giggled.

"Wouldn't it be great if we could change
the ballet to a comedy?" he heard one of them
say.

"Jenny's so good, I can't figure out why
she's dancing this way," another whispered
loudly.

Josh decided he had to relax. He checked
out Jenny in the mirror. Still cute as ever.
Now, if only he would move like he knew she
could.

"Shake it up, baby," he said aloud, to
Jenny, where ever she was. Where usually
Josh was a natural performer, he was now
self-conscious. These ballet movements felt
so unnatural.

"Jenny, I'm sure you'll be feeling a lot
better tomorrow," Mrs. Herbert fluttered
around her, leading Jenny off the floor so the
others could go on with rehearsal. "Why don't
you get a good night's sleep, practice if you
feel like it, and sit out the rest of class, all
right?"

"Yeah, okay," Josh said, relieved. But he
also felt bad for not being able to do right by
Jenny. Let's face it, Friedman, you bitched
it good. He turned to the bench that ran the
length of one wall.

He watched the others dance to the light,
airy music, noting how graceful they were.
Jessica Melvin, Tracy Holt, Sasha Hayward,
Amanda Sterling. The girls were all lean,

long-legged, and small-boned, but were each different in some way. They all danced expertly, but none of them, he decided, was as good as Jenny. Jenny's dancing was special, and that was probably why Mrs. Herbert was so upset.

Josh finished out the session, sitting slumped over while the students glided around the room. He tried to absorb as much information about dance as he could in that short time, listening carefully to Mrs. Herbert's instructions. Finally the lesson was over, and Mrs. Herbert excused everyone.

"Sorry we ended so late this evening, class," Mrs. Herbert frowned at her watch. "But we still have a few problems to iron out. See you tomorrow."

Jessica Melvin strode over. "Jenny, what's wrong? Are you sick?"

"Yeah, I guess so," Josh mumbled as he packed Jenny's ballet bag.

"I've never seen you so out of it," she said, her brow wrinkling in concern. Jessica was dark-haired, with long black lashes, and she was taller than the others.

"I should be better tomorrow, Jess. Thanks." Josh smiled, hoping there was some truth to his words.

He left with the rest of the class, wishing that their knowledge would magically rub off on him. Outside, everyone said good-bye.

"See you tomorrow, Jenny. Get some rest!" Jessica called, smiling sympathetically.

"Thanks, Jessica. I will."

Josh knew that Jessica was one of Jen's favorite people. There was naturally a lot of competition among the dancers, but they maintained a warm concern for each other. Since the five students had been chosen for this audition, the tension between dancers was heightened. They all knew that success for one meant failure for someone else. But they remained supportive of one another. Jenny said that was because they each knew what it was like to succeed, and to fail.

He waved good-bye, suddenly glad to get away from the others, whose concern felt uncomfortable. Girls sure did worry about one another, he thought. If this was a group of guys, they'd all be trading insults right now. The way guys softened the agony of defeat was by joking around, whereas girls were ready with a shoulder to cry on.

He started the Volkswagen, which spluttered a little. Maybe it sensed the change in its driver, Josh thought. He drove down the street, thinking about the fairy godfather. A little computer contact would be nice right now, he decided.

Josh had forgotten that as Jenny, he had chores to do. When he got to her house, Bernie was fixing dinner.

"I made pork chops," Bernie said, peering over the rim of his steamed-up glasses. "I didn't know when you would be home."

"I'm sorry. Dancing was kind of an ordeal today," Josh said.

"The health drink didn't help?" Bernie raised one eyebrow, but remained perfectly serious.

"Uh, no. I don't think its effects will show for a while." Smart kid, Josh thought to himself.

"I'm interested to see if health food makes a big difference in the way people perform," Bernie said, turning the chops onto a piece of paper towel. "Maybe I'll do a science project on it."

"Might be fun," Josh said distractedly, dragging open drawers in search of silverware. He found it and set the table. "You can use me as a guinea pig."

"You could show progress in leaps and bounds." Bernie smiled and handed Josh the chops.

"Cute, Bernie, real cute." Josh sat down at the table.

"I'll get Mom." Bernie ran off to the other end of the house.

Mrs. Knudson looked distracted when she came into the room.

"Hi, Jenny. How was rehearsal?" she asked, sitting down at the table.

"It was okay. Mrs. Herbert kept us longer than usual today, though."

"Oh?"

"Well, yeah. We had to go through the piece an extra time." He didn't say that the problems they had had were because of him.

"I thought something like that had happened when you came home late." Mrs. Knudson cut into her pork chop. She didn't eat it right away like Josh wanted to, so he felt self-conscious about giving in to his ravenous impulses.

"How was school?" he asked her.

"Fine. I lectured on 'Humor in our Society.'" Mrs. Knudson taught a popular culture course at the local university.

"Hear any good jokes?" Josh inquired.

"No, I *told* them, Jenny. And analyzed them — topical jokes, news-item jokes, ethnic jokes, political jokes. The list is endless. And then you have the pun."

"A mother who tells jokes for a living. Wild." Josh tasted his food.

"What was once offensive is now humorous," Mrs. Knudson continued, as though she had never stopped giving her lecture. "But mostly I talked about trends in jokes, such as computer jokes, for instance."

"Computer jokes?" Every fiber of Josh's being was alerted at the mention of the word computer.

"Yes. Such as a recent magazine cartoon that shows a man on his deathbed, and the doctor turns to the nurse and says, 'Call in the family, I think he's about to process his last words.'"

Bernie and Josh laughed.

"Just imagine if we got to the point where we didn't communicate any longer, except through computers," Bernie suggested. He started to clear the table when they had finished eating.

Josh got up to help, knowing Jenny would.

"I mean, what if a person appeared on the computer screen every morning, and you just told him what you wanted done for the day, and it was done?" Bernie went on.

"Have you seen such a person on a computer screen lately?" Josh quizzed him hopefully. Maybe the fairy godfather was a regular. Maybe he had already introduced himself to other members of the family!

Bernie laughed. "Only in my imagination. What I would give to see that. Someone who would make life so easy."

"Yes, well that would be nice. But there's no guarantee this person would make life easy," said Josh knowingly. "Are you sure you haven't noticed anything weird about the computer lately?"

Frowning, Bernie wagged his head. "No, of course not. Hey, Jen, you're not taking this seriously, are you?"

Josh squirmed. "Uh, oh, no. I might be able to use this idea for an English assignment, though," he said, to cover himself.

Mrs. Knudson rose from the table. "It all sounds so farfetched, you two. If you'll excuse me, I'm off to correct papers."

Bernie and Josh cleared the dishes and loaded the dishwasher. Then Josh passed by the den to see if it was free, but Mrs. Knudson was working in that room. He would have to wait.

Every muscle in Josh's body ached as he went into Jenny's room to do her homework.

It was already eight o'clock, but he sat at her desk and waded diligently through her work until it was finished.

Josh found Jenny's nightgowns without much trouble (she was pretty tidy). As he got dressed for bed, he wondered why they had ever argued about sex. Why didn't Jenny want him? She said she loved him, but then sometimes, just her distance, her distractedness, made him think otherwise, even though he wouldn't admit it to anyone. He felt pushed along by a force that wouldn't let up. He wanted her, it was that simple. So why couldn't she feel the same way about him? He felt like *he* was the one doing all the wanting.

Well, that whole question was on hold now. He tiptoed down the hall to see if Mrs. Knudson was still in the den.

She wasn't. He turned on the light and sat down at the computer. He loaded the game diskette, and whispered, "Come on, Fairy Godfather, don't let me down. I need to talk to you, now!"

Josh hoped the urgency in his voice would bring up the face, but the godfather didn't appear. Josh played three games while waiting for him. In despair, Josh switched off the computer and trudged back to Jenny's bedroom.

Chapter 7

Jenny stood in the shower and let the water stream over Josh's body and tried to relax. Relaxation doesn't come easily, she thought, when every moment you are aware of the fact that you aren't yourself. Around Josh's friends she had to be him. And now, even in the shower, where she usually enjoyed the solitude, there was the disturbing presence of Josh's body. She wanted to be back in *her* body — she wanted to be alone.

She stepped out of the shower and dressed quickly in a pair of faded cords and a shirt she'd never seen Josh wear before. The shirt had been shoved to the back of one of his drawers, and Jenny was immediately taken with its blurred brown-and-blue stripes.

Then she went into the kitchen to see what was for dinner. There was a quiche on top of the stove, with a note underneath.

> *Mrs. Friedman,*
> *Cook at 350° for about 25 minutes.*
> *There's a salad in the refrigerator.*
> *—Betsy*

Jenny located the salad and decided to make some dressing for it. Mrs. Friedman wasn't due home until around six, and Jenny found herself with plenty of time, which was rare for her.

She put a load of Josh's laundry in the washer and set to work on the dressing. Then she started on Josh's homework.

Josh's desk was piled high with papers. As far as he was concerned, he could find his way around in the mess just fine, but Jenny had a little trouble. She cleared the surface and organized the work space a little better.

While cleaning up, a few small, parchment-thin sheets of paper sailed to the carpet, fanning out in a stunning display of artwork that caused Jenny to gasp with surprise.

She bent to carefully pick up the papers. There was a sketch of a group of sailboats, done in pen and ink with a fine gray wash. The next one was a self-portrait of Josh in his baseball uniform. Then there was one of a couple of boys running down the block. Jenny ran her finger along the casual, free-flowing lines of Josh's drawing, thinking about him.

Never before had she seen any of Josh's work like this stuff. Jenny knew he was a good artist. He was spontaneous, breezy about anything he did artistically. He was casual, never worried, and his work turned out great, but never *this* great. These sketches had the same spontaneity as the work she'd seen before, but they were reinforced by bold, assertive strokes that held her eye.

Jenny studied the drawings for a long while, absorbing Josh's personality from them. She felt momentarily annoyed that he had never shared these with her, when she often asked to see what he was working on. But he had a tendency to shrug off his talent, change the subject, or distract her in any number of ways.

Gazing around the comfortable but cluttered room, she found herself wishing she could be easier about things, like Josh. Her life *was* more demanding than his, mostly of her own choosing, yet she made it seem even more so. Dance was at the center of it all. She was always busy, always on a tight schedule. So what really irked her was when Josh behaved as though missing her dance class was nothing to get upset about. He didn't take her ambition or her emotions seriously — he was always the one to say, "Calm down, life isn't going anywhere without you."

"It might," Jenny was fond of saying, because she really believed if she didn't keep pace with her internal clock, somehow the entire Jenny Knudson system would break down.

But now, there was absolutely nothing she could do about it. She certainly couldn't keep pace with her clock when she wasn't in touch with her own body.

Sighing, Jenny slipped the drawings carefully into a drawer and did some of Josh's homework. Then at a quarter to six, she went into the kitchen to turn on the oven. Mrs. Friedman walked in just as she was putting in the quiche.

"Josh, thank you!" she exclaimed, depositing a kiss on her son's cheek. "How did you know, I'm absolutely starved?"

"I heard your stomach growling three miles down the road," Jenny joked. Pretty good, she commended herself. A Josh comment if ever there was one.

"Yes, well." She sailed through the laundry room on the way to the bathroom. "How long ago did Betsy leave? There's laundry in here."

"I put that load in, Mom." Jenny felt strange calling Mrs. Friedman "Mom."

"My God! Are you all right? Are you having an attack of neatness or something?" she cried.

"Well, uh, my gym clothes needed washing." That was at least true.

Mrs. Friedman chuckled. "They usually do."

Mr. Friedman strolled in from work, raising one dark eyebrow at his son, who stood at the kitchen sink. He was a large, bearish-looking man with a full beard.

"Josh in the kitchen? I'd better take a picture of this," Mr. Friedman remarked.

"I know it's foreign territory for me, but I wanted to start dinner early," Jenny explained.

"Either you've got a date, or you want a new piece of baseball equipment," Mr. Friedman teased.

"No, it's just me, being a good kid," Jenny responded, realizing that all this was out of character for Josh. Josh was kind of spoiled, but not in a bad way. He just wasn't expected to do much around the house, so he didn't.

Over dinner, Mrs. Friedman exclaimed about the salad dressing. "Where'd you learn to make this, Josh? I always thought you had trouble boiling water."

"They taught us how to do this at camp, Mom," Jenny replied, figuring that was a pretty good answer. She knew Josh knew how to cook camp food. They'd talked about that before. Yet she had no idea if he'd ever made a vinaigrette dressing. She knew he'd heated up a lot of Ravioli-O's, but needless to say, he wasn't exactly a gourmet.

"Oh, right, I forgot. It's just that your culinary expertise has never been apparent in this house before," Mrs. Friedman joked.

"Give him credit, Rachel," scoffed Mr. Friedman. "He *is* your only child."

"I know and I worry about him, Sid," she sighed. ". . . with all the stories you hear. You know, my 'Living with a Teen' class is really a great education. They say learning begins at home, but I'm not so sure."

It seemed strange to Jenny that Mrs. Friedman took a class to teach her how to live with a teenager. "If you want to learn how to live with a teen, Mom, why don't you just ask me?"

"Pardon me?" she blinked in surprise. "Oh, I suppose I could, but I like hearing what the experts think."

"You worry too much. I'm not in trouble. I'm pretty clean, you know," Jenny said reassuringly.

"Uh, I think you'd better rephrase that, son." Mr. Friedman leaned over to whisper. "Your mother can argue that point by taking a look in your bedroom."

Which I'm going to fix, thought Jenny. I can't live in that chaos, even for three days.

"Well, today it was the Nordstroms' son, Willis. He's talking about running away from home." Mrs. Friedman folded her napkin carefully and stood up.

"Maybe he doesn't get fed well enough," suggested Mr. Friedman, trying to be light. "The Nordstroms are on one of those macrobiotic diets, aren't they?"

"Don't worry, Mom. I'm not leaving home — as long as you feed me, that is," Jenny put in.

She smiled but she was still serious. "You don't know what a relief that is, Josh, really."

Jenny got up and helped load the dishwasher, which was another source of surprise to Mr. and Mrs. Friedman.

"Just don't put any soap in the machine, Josh," Mrs. Friedman cautioned. "Remember what happened the last time you did that?"

"Oh, yeah. Right." Jenny backed away from the dishwasher in confusion. Just what *had* happened the last time Josh had used the machine? Knowing Josh. . . .

Finally, the Friedmans drifted off to watch television, and Jenny went up to Josh's room.

Exhaustion was ready to overtake her. The day had been probably the hardest of her life, and she was too tired for homework. She turned off the bedside light and lay in the dark, listening to the way breath sounded inhaling from Josh's body. She listened until it sounded familiar to her.

She thought of how affectionate Josh was, always wanting them to touch, be closer, to be more physical. Well, Jenny wanted to, too; it wasn't a one-way street. But sometimes, when they were together, her love for him was so overwhelming that she became frightened. A huge new intimacy would be a major step. She was afraid it would change their feelings for each other. Josh's impatience caused her to back off, and she found it difficult to explain to him why she wasn't ready. Now she wondered what made it different for boys. Was sex more important to them? Were boys just ready for it earlier than girls?

Friday, Josh and Jenny muddled through the morning hours at home. Then Jenny picked up Josh and they rode to school together.

For Josh, the morning had been fraught

with problems. Mrs. Knudson had asked him to fix pancakes, which Josh didn't know how to do. So he had mixed up the batter according to the instructions and had poured it into a Dutch oven. Bernie had come to the rescue, spooning it out and putting blobs into a buttered frying pan.

"Jenny, what's wrong with you?" Bernie had frowned. "You've always made the greatest pancakes."

"I have?" Josh had blinked in amazement. "Uh, yes, I have," he had amended quickly.

"Yeah, I can't figure it out. Watch out, you're going to burn those."

Clumsily, Josh had hiked the pancakes out of the pan onto a plate. He had felt so incompetent. He really had to learn to cook, he told Jenny later.

Then Jenny's mother had become exasperated because someone, namely Josh, had put too much detergent in the dishwasher and it had bubbled over, down the front of the machine onto the floor. There had been bits of detergent stuck to the dishes inside, the dog had tracked suds across the floor, and everything had had to be cleaned again.

Jenny's story was an altogether different one. Apparently, Mrs. Friedman had been happily horrified to find Josh had cleaned up his room. That was so unlike him!

"We have to be more alike," Josh said, as he and Jenny drove to school.

"Maybe we ought to trade genes next," Jenny joked.

"Don't make a wish," Josh said, and they both laughed.

"Well, I *do* wish I hadn't missed dance class yesterday," Jenny continued. "How was the rehearsal?"

"Don't ask," moaned Josh. "I'm a pretty athletic guy, but ballet's not my thing. Class was late getting out because of me, and good old Bernie had dinner ready when I got home." Josh looked a little sheepish. "Sorry."

"Oh, Josh," Jenny bit her lip, remembering exactly how she had felt after her baseball experience in his body. "What did Mrs. Herbert say?"

"She just worried about my health. And about whether I was going to be able to make the audition." Josh whistled through his teeth.

Jenny sympathized. "Look, don't feel bad about dance. It's not your fault. I've played baseball before but you've never been a ballet student. Even so, I made a mess of things. The coach thinks you're sick, and he said he has never seen you play so badly. . . ."

"Geez, this could jeopardize my position on the team," he said thoughtfully.

"Look, maybe today we'll reach the fairy godfather," Jenny suggested. "If he's stuck in that computer, he must have to make human contact — to eat, don't you think?"

"Maybe. Although he might be a self-contained being and not need food."

"Like a ghost," Jenny agreed.

"Yeah, sort of," Josh added.

"I don't like the idea of my life being in the hands of some ghostly being," said Jenny.

"It's just a theory, Jen. I mean he could be anything — we really don't have any idea *what* he is. Look, after dance class let's take a quick break. Let's go to a movie," he suggested. "That way, we won't have to pretend to each other for awhile. We can just be ourselves."

"Sounds good to me," Jenny sighed with relief.

But for the rest of the day, school occupied Jenny's thoughts. Computer science left her completely in the dark. Where the day before Mr. Leipzig hadn't really looked at Josh's spread sheets, today he checked assignments. Jenny knew absolutely nothing about spread sheets. And there was no opportunity for her to find a free computer to try to contact the fairy godfather.

Worse yet, Coach Jacobs called a special baseball practice session after school. The boys met on the field. Josh's friends continued ribbing him about his baseball practice. "And then running out of the gym, man, you were totally out of it," one of the boys said.

At practice Jenny assured the team, "Today will be better."

"Yeah, tell us about it, Friedman," someone said.

So there was the challenge. Jenny was filled with anger and purpose. They were baiting Josh, setting him up — if you fail, you're a loser. So much for team support.

Jenny strode up to bat, trying to walk like Josh, imagining that she *was* him. Okay, Josh, she thought as she crouched, this time we'll show them. We'll blot out the memory of yesterday.

"Strike one!" the coach yelled. Jenny tottered a little from the force of her swing. "Choke up on that bat, Friedman. Thata boy."

One voice of encouragement. She leaned forward in determination. "Ball one!" Come on, come on, Josh, let's show them how. . . .

Crack! The ball flew off into left field. Jenny dropped the bat and ran, sliding into first base. Everyone cheered.

The next two players struck out, and Jenny took Josh's field position on first base. She caught two fly balls. Eyes viewed Josh with renewed respect. The coach waved his fist enthusiastically.

"Looks like I've redeemed myself," Jenny told the pitcher, Willie Edwards, afterward.

"What're you talking about, Friedman? This is a team, you know? Everybody always does his best."

"Or else," Jenny muttered. But she couldn't explain to any of them what she was feeling. Marooned. Alone with failure, and even attacked. Not like when she had a bad day dancing, and the other girls were nurturing, concerned about her. They helped each other with disappointments.

"You're not allowed to make mistakes, are

you?" Jenny commented to Josh later when they were on their way to a movie.

"What do you mean?" Josh seemed puzzled by the question.

"I mean, your teammates show no concern for your feelings if you mess up. Whatever's wrong you'd better fix, or joke yourself out of it."

"I never noticed." Josh shrugged.

"Girls share their pain, and boys don't," Jenny said simply.

Josh remembered Jessica's concern for Jenny after rehearsal. "Guys are not into weakness," he said.

"Is pain weakness?" Jenny questioned.

"It is to guys," Josh responded, but he looked distracted. "Hey, look, a parking space right in front of the theater."

"They also like to change the subject," Jenny noted ruefully.

"Come on, we don't have a lot of time." Anxiously, he scooted out of the car. Jenny knew this was the end of the conversation.

She lagged behind, thinking about those rare times when Josh did confide in her. Then it was as though she was the only person in the world who knew intimate things about him. He divulged information about his family, his fears, but not how he felt about her. He told her he loved her, but he never said more on the subject. Sometimes he told her he wanted her.

Josh didn't really have a need to be very revealing, Jenny realized. He naturally kept things to himself. He didn't seem to worry about emotions. Often, Jenny wondered just where he put them all, or maybe it was that they just showed themselves in different ways than she expected.

"Hey, Jen, are you coming?" he called across the lot. A couple of people did a double take. Jenny giggled, hurrying to catch us. It struck her suddenly as funny, ludicrously funny, to watch him in her body, gesturing wildly.

When she came closer, he slipped an arm around her. "What're you laughing at? People will think you've lost your mind," he cautioned.

"They may be right," she said. "My mind is trapped in the body of a madman."

"You say the sweetest things to me sometimes," Josh joked.

They laughed and strolled into the theater — just like old times.

Chapter 8

The next morning Josh switched on the computer. He heard Bernie come in, so he turned it off and went out to meet him.

"What's for dinner tonight?" asked Bernie.

"Uh, I haven't thought about it," stuttered Josh. His thoughts were still back in the den.

Bernie peered into the refrigerator. "If you think you'll be late again, we can have chili dogs. They're easy."

"Uh, okay," Josh figured it was best not to argue. If Bernie thought they were easy to make, then they must be. "Hey, Bernie."

"Huh?" Bernie blinked at him, his mouth around a brownie.

"Will you fix them for me?"

"That's your job, Jen. I made dinner last night.

"Yeah, I know. But I will be really squeezed for time. Rehearsals are longer this week," and then I have plans to go to town with Josh." Josh knew he was pushing his luck but he went with it anyway. "I'll do something for you."

"Like what?" Bernie sighed.

"Uh, feed your hamster, maybe?"

"Okay, we'll work something out. I'll fix dinner. Oh!" Bernie snatched a note off the refrigerator door. "Don't forget to pick up some milk, okay?"

"Okay," called Josh as he sped out the door, then ran back in to grab a sweatshirt at the last minute. There was so much to remember! It was hard trying to keep Jenny's life straight.

The grocery store, dinner, dishes, dancing — how did she do it all? Not to mention homework. She was amazing, absolutely amazing. It had never occurred to Josh before that she had so much to do, even though she mentioned it from time to time.

His own life was easy, he reflected, as he rode Jenny's bike down toward the dance studio. He knew other girls didn't have as much responsibility as Jenny, it was just circumstances that put her in this position. Well, not entirely, he corrected himself. If she didn't have ballet, she'd have a lot less to contend with.

When Josh strode into the studio, the other girls glanced up to say hi. There was a new girl in the group who was introduced to him as Caitlin Tapper.

"Jenny, how's it going?" Jessica asked. She wore two different-colored leg warmers, one bright pink, the other green, with a bright orange-striped leotard and purple tights. Josh thought she looked like a Pop Art exhibit, all on one canvas. He was so stunned by her colors it took him a minute to answer. "Jenny?" Jessica looked at her friend expectantly.

"Oh, uh, fine," Josh breathed nervously.

"I'm getting really excited, aren't you?" Jessica added.

"Yeah." Josh wasn't sure excited was the right word to describe what he was feeling. The other girls were now congregated around a box of white tutus, leotards, and tights, which formed the basis for their costumes for the recital. Excitement was definitely in the air.

"We'll be wearing white tutus and toe shoes, which will look really great," Jessica went on. "I want to see the stage beforehand, just so I can visualize how we'll all look."

"Sounds wonderful," Josh said, but Jenny's voice came out flat. He had never thought much about ballet costumes before. "I guess this is like getting new baseball uniforms," he remarked.

Jessica frowned. "What? Oh, I guess so. But why would you care about that, Jen? You're not into baseball now, are you?"

"Well, uh, not exactly. My brother is," Josh lied.

"Oh."

Jessica handed Josh a white leotard, tutu, and matching tights. "Here, you wear a small. These ought to fit."

Just then Mrs. Herbert clapped her hands together to signal the beginning of class.

Obediently, Josh took Jenny's place at the barre and began with the preliminary exercises.

"Jennifer, your second position looks more like a straddle. Bring your feet together, dear."

Josh did as Jenny was told. He concentrated on being her, on what the others were doing. It was paying off. Mrs. Herbert didn't watch Jenny much during the first part of class. The new student, Caitlin Tapper, commanded her attention at the other end of the barre. Later, Josh heard Mrs. Herbert tell Caitlin that she should be in a different class because this was a little too advanced for her.

Thank goodness for new students, thought Josh, as he went through the bolder movements of the next dance.

"Jenny, watch those jumps! You're off balance!" cried Mrs. Herbert in exasperation.

Josh tottered to a halt, just in time to see Caitlin disappear out the studio door. That meant Mrs. Herbert would direct her full focus back to him.

The instructor came over to him, and in a low, confidential tone she said, "This is where everyone will be watching you, Jennifer. You are the principal dancer, so the audience naturally follows you. Remember, you are to be exuberant, but not so wild."

She went on explaining. "You must be

exquisite, perfect. The last couple of days you have not danced your best, but then you know that." Mrs. Herbert patted Josh's arm. "Practice, my dear, practice until your heart aches."

"Yeah, sure, okay." Josh had forgotten about practicing. He had been thinking only of himself — of baseball practices he was missing, of his own life, from which he was absent. Practice would help here, definitely. After all, he probably could do better. Maybe if he tried to think more like Jenny, be her for the day. . . .

He went through the routine, carefully this time, concentrating. Jenny was the most important dancer. Even an untrained observer like himself could tell that. He remembered how beautiful she had been in the last performance he had seen; how, even though she had an ordinary part, she had shone brighter than the other girls. Her talent was special, open, and natural. Could he copy that talent? It was impossible, wasn't it? He figured her body knew the language — if only her mind was there to lead it. If Josh had her knowledge right now, the dance would be perfect.

"Much better, Jennifer! Much, much better! You are still a little forceful in places. Not so much flinging of the arms, love." Mrs. Herbert's twiglike fingers darted in the air. "I think you will recover in time for our performance." Her smile was encouraging.

"I sure hope so," Josh responded, grinning. Recover was just the right word for it. He wondered if there was a standard recuperation period for body-switchers.

After class, Jessica asked Jenny if she wanted to go out for a Coke.

Josh hedged. "Uh, I don't know. . . ."

"You always have something to do after class. Although I do understand. But we did make plans last week," Jessica pointed out.

Josh thought about all the chores that had to be done at home. And then he thought about how hard it would be to turn Jessica down. He didn't want to mess around with Jenny's friendships.

"Sure, let's go, but just for a little while," he said.

Josh packed Jenny's canvas ballet bag and followed Jessica out of the studio. They went across the street to a coffee shop, whose front windows were filled with hanging plants and seashell mobiles.

Josh ordered a milk shake. He took the straw out of the glass and laid it on his napkin.

Jessica eyed her friend strangely, but continued to sip at her ice-cream soda. "You know, your dancing has changed in the last couple of days. I can tell you haven't practiced, but something else is different."

"Oh?" Fear swelled in Josh's throat.

Jessica pressed her fingertip against her lower lip. "Masculine. That's what it is. Your dancing seems masculine all of a sudden.

It's not exactly clumsy, just masculine."

"What do you mean by that?" Josh gulped.

"Well, there is a difference, as you know, Jen." Jessica smiled. "More aggressiveness than grace."

"That sounds sort of sexist," Josh remarked, frowning.

"Oh, come on. We've been in dance classes together since we were nine years old. We've seen both boys and girls dance. While men and women are equal, they're definitely different in how they perform."

"Yeah, I guess you're right. But there's nothing wrong with dancing like a guy," said Josh defensively. "Nobody complains about Mikhail Baryshnikov dancing like a guy."

"Nothing wrong with it at all," Jessica nodded. "As long as you're not a girl."

Josh nearly gagged on his milk shake, but he tried to be cool. "Maybe I'll start a new trend," he suggested.

Jessica leaned across the table. "Is there anything bothering you, Jenny?" she asked. "Maybe you need to talk."

"Bothering me? Oh, no!" Josh denied, wagging Jenny's head ferociously. "I'm fine."

"Well, you know you can tell me if there is. I don't think we've had a good talk in a long time."

"No, I guess we haven't." Hey, maybe never, Josh thought, smiling. He didn't feel comfortable with this attempt at sharing confidences. Why do girls always want to *talk*?

He tapped his straw against a spoon, trying to figure out a good way to exit this conversation and restaurant.

"Hey, listen, I've gotta go, Jessica. I've made plans with Josh. You understand, right?"

"Yeah, sure." Jessica looked disappointed, but she accepted Josh's explanation.

Josh couldn't get out of there fast enough. He tripped over chair legs as he left, feeling suddenly too light. Sure, Jenny's body had felt that way to him all along, but right then it seemed to soar, weightless, with him inside it. He could feel Jessica's eyes on Jenny's back as he scrambled for the door, which made him even more nervous.

Yet once he was away from her, Jessica's words took root in Josh's mind. Maybe his masculinity kept him from expressing Jenny's way of dancing. Then again, he didn't know *how* to be feminine. Even from the time they were little kids, boys were discouraged from doing anything "girlish."

He figured if he could tune into Jenny's femininity somehow, and practice for hours like she did, maybe, just maybe, he could pull off this dance rehearsal. That is, if he and Jenny were stuck this way through tomorrow, as well.

"I forgot to tell you," Jenny said, while she and Josh walked along Main Street later. "You're going to a slumber party tonight at Elyse's house. I'm sorry."

"A slumber party? D'you mean all girls?"

"Well, sure," she said confusedly. "So far, our parents haven't allowed us to invite boys."

"I'm not going," he declared without hesitation. He stopped in front of a computer store.

"You have to, Josh," Jenny argued.

"No, I don't," Josh retorted. "That's above and beyond the call of duty."

"No one will understand if I don't show up."

"I'm not going to sit around and listen to them talk about clothes and boys and who knows what else." Josh sounded firm.

"That isn't *all* girls talk about, Josh, and you know it," Jenny coaxed.

"I don't know it, and I don't *want* to know. I just want to be myself for a while," he replied.

"Well, you're not the only one." Jenny said angrily, catching Josh's arm. "This is important to Elyse. She's been planning it for weeks, and I'm her best friend."

"So I'm stuck?" Josh sighed. "Can't I come down with some rare disease or anything?"

"I don't think that's funny," said Jenny.

Josh whistled. This was worse than what he'd undergone so far. "What do you do at those things, anyway? I always wondered. Guys just don't have slumber parties."

Jenny laughed with relief. "It's not much different from when we were little kids at camp. Remember when you stayed up late and told ghost stories and had pillow fights? We talk and laugh. I'm sorry I'm going to miss it."

"Me, too. Hey, look, is that a face in that computer?" Josh suddenly caught sight of a graph image in one of the computers displayed in a store window.

Jenny turned to see the face only to find it was just a cartoon onscreen. "What a disappointment!" she cried.

"Let's go inside," he suggested. She followed Josh inside the store, where he asked about the computer in the window. "You don't have a program that shows human faces, do you?"

The shopkeeper laughed. "No, but I'm sure someone will come out with such a model in a couple of years."

Jenny and Josh looked at each other. "I'm afraid that will be too late," Jenny said quietly.

Josh sat down and asked how to operate the cartoon program. The clerk was happy to give him a demonstration, then left them alone.

"If we can make contact with the fairy godfather and get changed back now, then I don't have to go to your slumber party," Josh said eagerly.

"And I can go myself," she concluded.

Fifteen minutes later, the sales clerk was back. "Is there anything else I can help you with? Do you want to buy this system?" he asked.

"No, thanks," said Josh quickly. It was fun to play with the new computer, but the fairy godfather was not being cooperative. Jenny and Josh thanked the clerk and trudged outside with fistfuls of fliers.

"Well, so much for that. He's not in the dream machine."

"Now I almost don't believe I ever saw him," Jenny shook her head. "I don't think he really exists anymore. It was a dream."

"Then so is this situation. The only consolation is that tomorrow morning the three days are up. We should wake up as ourselves."

"At least I'll get to wake up at Elyse's house," Jenny said.

Josh consulted Jenny's watch. "It's a quarter to six."

"You have a party to go to at seven-thirty."

Josh groaned. "What'll I wear?"

"Just jeans — it's not formal. And bring a nightgown."

"Anything else I need to know?"

Jenny giggled. "You should be fine. If you get stuck, call me, okay?"

"Okay." They stopped at the end of the street and kissed, then went in opposite directions.

As Josh walked toward Jenny's house, he began to daydream about various ways of avoiding Elyse's party. He could make contact with the fairy godfather. He could have an accident and get amnesia. He could get sick. He could disappear.

He rounded the corner in view of Jenny's house, and saw Elyse's car parked in the drive. His heart dropped like a stone. He was caught, and none of the possibilities he'd considered would work now.

Josh Friedman was clearly destined to attend a girls' slumber party.

Chapter 9

"Hi, Jenny!" Elyse called out gaily when she caught sight of her friend.

"Hi," Josh replied stiffly. He breathed deeply. Okay, you're going through with this. Now Friedman, just do your best.

Elyse fell in step beside him as he walked toward the house. "I was in the neighborhood, so I decided to come get you. Have you packed already?"

"Uh, no, but it won't take a minute." Usually, when Josh went anywhere overnight, he only took his toothbrush and an extra T-shirt to sleep in. In Jenny's room, Elyse watched while he selected a nightgown, zipped up a yellow totebag, and grabbed Jenny's sleeping bag.

"Is that all you're bringing?" she asked. "No makeup or extra clothes?"

"No, this is all. I'm only staying the night, remember?"

Elyse blinked in confusion and then said, "Oh, you can borrow something of mine if you need to. . . . Come on, the others are probably there already. Let's hurry, before they eat all the food."

Josh typed a note for Bernie and Mrs. Knudson, and followed Elyse out to her car. This was all happening so fast.

"How many of us will be there?" Josh asked.

"Oh, you know, Jenny! Me, you, Connie, Toni, and Cathy. The usual crowd." Elyse breezed through the intersection and turned up her street.

Josh felt like asking a lot of questions, but he figured he should know everything there was to know about the party, so he kept quiet. If this were *his* best friend, he reflected, they would be talking about baseball probably, and they sure wouldn't be getting together for a reason like this.

The other girls were in the backyard when they arrived at Elyse's house. With Connie in the lead, they came over to the side entrance to see who was arriving.

"Oh, Jen, hi!" Everyone crowded around. "We were doing handstands in the back-yard."

"Hi."

Bits of newly mowed grass clung to their hair and clothes. Josh felt awkward for a moment, but then Connie whisked away Jen's bag, and led her friend into the backyard.

Elyse's yard was huge, bordered on all sides by flowerbeds, and in the center was a volleyball net.

"Show us how to do handstands, Jen!" urged Toni.

"She's into standing on her toes, not her hands," Connie said.

"It happens that I'm pretty talented upside down," Josh said, demonstrating his skill as a gymnast by walking across the garden on Jenny's hands.

The girls clapped. Toni tried a backbend. "Let me show you how," Josh offered, holding the center of her back and letting her curve around it. "That's right — you've got it!"

"Really? How do you know? By the pain?" she asked, grimacing.

"Let's eat something," Elyse interrupted. "I think we've worked up appetites."

Everyone gravitated toward the house. A buffet was set up in the dining room. Josh picked up a piece of shrimp and popped it in his mouth.

"High-gloss food." Toni waved a piece of salami in the air.

"There's a pizza, too," Elyse added.

"Is this a celebration of some kind? A birthday, maybe?" Josh asked.

"No major event. Just getting together, Jen." Cathy frowned. "This isn't your first slumber party, remember?"

"Oh, right." Josh smiled benignly. Remember, this is *not* your first slumber party, he told himself. Act as though this is normal for you, jerk. The expressions on the girls' faces registered brief puzzlement, but conversation quickly moved on to food and old times.

Then Elyse put on a record. Some of the girls began to dance. Josh stood by the food, eating.

"Come on, Jen, let's dance," Connie pulled her friend out onto the floor, with pizza in one hand.

It always amazed Josh how girls danced together. They never seemed to mind. Boys would never do that, he thought. They would be too afraid of what other guys would think.

"I was reading a ballerina's journal in the library yesterday," Cathy said. "She described how she felt about dancing — that it's her whole life. Is that how it is for you, Jenny?"

What was it like? Josh knew dance played a big part in Jen's life. It seemed different than sports were to him. He liked many different sports, whereas Jenny was focused on ballet. "Yeah, it is," he answered finally. "I think about it all the time."

Josh didn't realize until he said those words that they were true. Jenny probably *did* think about dance all the time. He'd certainly thought about it a lot since he'd become her.

"When you're dancing, you look like you're part of a dream," Cathy sighed.

I *feel* like I'm part of a dream, Josh reflected. "That's how I'm supposed to look. You work real hard at looking unreal."

"Do you really have to spend as much time as you do practicing?" questioned Cathy.

The other girls stopped dancing and gathered around. This was a question Josh had asked Jenny countless times. He said yes, because he figured that was the only answer Jenny would give. He'd certainly heard her say it enough.

"I think it's wonderful to be so involved in something, and know that it will be your career, your whole life," Cathy said.

The group moved to clean up the food, eating more in the process. Then sleeping bags were rolled out on the living room carpet. All this, just to get together and sleep and talk, Josh reflected. They talked about grades and about colleges they thought they wanted to go to.

"I think I want to apply to a school in the East just so I can live somewhere else and meet new people," explained Toni. "I've lived in this town all my life."

"I think it's a good idea," Elyse said. "But I would miss home too much. I think I'm better off staying here."

"Since my father's been sick, I've wanted to stay close, said Cathy. "Although breaking up with Doug has made me dream about living far away."

"You won't always feel this way, though," Elyse reminded her.

Josh went into the bathroom and changed into Jenny's nightgown, but came back in time to hear more:

"I don't know what I'd do without you guys, really," Cathy said softly.

"We ought to market our secret, whatever it is," said Toni.

"Fun Incorporated," Elyse joked.

"Elixir for a Heartbreak," Connie offered, and the girls laughed.

"Laughter is the best medicine, they say," Elyse offered, adding, " — and time heals all wounds."

"A rolling stone gathers no moss," Josh joked, and everyone laughed again.

"What happened with Doug has made me appreciate Carl more," Elyse said to Cathy. "I mean, you think you're going to stay together forever because you feel a certain way, but it doesn't always happen."

"Why not?" Cathy asked.

"Because people change," Elyse replied. "You can't count on staying the same, that's what my older sister says."

There were tears in Cathy's eyes. "That's what happened with us. I was always trying to please him in every way, but that didn't make either of us happy. Doug wanted more space."

"Guys talk about space a lot," Elyse said. "They want their independence, and are afraid girls want to take it away."

"Some girls do," Toni claimed. "I just want to be really close to a guy, talk about anything under the sun, share everything," she declared.

"What about sex?" Josh asked. He had forgotten who he was supposed to be, intent on this conversation.

"What about it? It's only a part of the whole relationship," Cathy said. "Sometimes, I think boys think it's more important than girls do, though."

"Maybe they think sex is love," Elyse guessed.

"When I say I want to be close, Alex doesn't realize that I don't necessarily mean *that* kind of close," Connie said. "I mean talking, sharing, laughing together."

"It seemed like Doug couldn't think of anything but sex when we were together," Cathy intimated. "We fought over that a lot. I felt pressured."

Josh listened to this conversation in wonderment. Did sex mean more to guys? Did they really think about it the way these girls described? He wasn't sure, because most of his friends were like himself — they just didn't talk about their feelings.

"Boys don't realize we feel differently about it," said Elyse. "We want to be romantic. The relationship is more important. We want to know that we're loved."

"It's hard to tell if a boy really loves you. Sometimes they don't say so," Connie added.

"I need to hear the words once in a while," Toni said.

Cathy turned to Jenny. "You're not saying much, Jenny."

"I'm just thinking," Josh replied uncertainly.

"About Josh, I'll bet?"

"Yes, and about Jenny."

Everyone giggled. Maybe some confidence was expected of Jenny, some word that this was her experience with Josh, too. He was amazed at the openness of the girls, and frightened by it. Did Jenny talk to her friends about *him* this way? And if so, how could he ever share anything with her without it becoming common knowledge?

He felt annoyed by all the girls' complaints about boys. What was all this talk about love and sex, anyway? It sounded like boys and girls were always upset with each other, never agreeing on anything. "Sex can be an expression of love," he blurted out suddenly. "What's wrong with that?"

The girls were startled. "Jenny, are you trying to tell us something?" Cathy asked slowly.

Josh realized what Jenny had just said, and felt embarrassed. "Boys think differently than you think they do. They have feelings, too, but they don't sit around and talk about them this way, that's all."

"I'm sure you're right, but I wish we could climb inside their heads for a day," Elyse said.

"Don't say that," Josh said quickly. If they only knew, he thought. Wishing is no joking matter.

As the conversation died away, he snuggled down in Jenny's sleeping bag, and Elyse turned out the lights. The murmur of the girls' voice faded, and Josh considered the whole evening from his very special viewpoint. He thought about holding Jenny, about the mixture of desire and fear that ran through him, and he realized something new. That girls were afraid, perhaps more cautious in their approach toward sex. It didn't mean they were being cruel or thoughtless, and it wasn't a sign of rejection, as he had thought it was with Jenny. They wanted to be loved — they wanted to be sure of that.

That night, Josh went to sleep with a lot on his mind. He dreamed he and Jenny were in their own bodies again, but every time they didn't understand each other, the fairy godfather made them change places. Once during the night, Josh awoke in a cold sweat. Then he looked around him at the lumpy outlines of Jenny's friends. Finally, assured that he'd only been dreaming, he fell back into a fitful sleep.

Chapter 10

At 6:30 that same night, Terry Fields honked for Josh outside of Josh's house. Jenny yelled out the window for Terry to wait, as she tried to wrench Josh's body into his wetsuit. Terry had called moments before to remind Josh that they had a date to go surfing. Jenny grabbed his surfboard as she hurried out of his room, then raced to the driveway and then stuck it in the back of Terry's station wagon. She wished she knew how to surf, because she was more than a little nervous, and who wanted to surf at night?

"It's about time. Thought you were gonna chicken out. We'll have a good hour of daylight to surf in."

Terry drove down the street, and onto the main road through town. He gunned the engine as they passed three girls jogging along the side of the road. He stepped on the brakes and backed up, thrusting his head out the window. "Wanna ride?" he yelled.

Jenny wanted to crawl under the seat. She

always thought it was weird that Josh hung out with somebody like Terry. They didn't seem a bit alike.

"No, thanks!" The girls yelled back.

"I give healthy rides — lots of oxygen," Terry said. Jenny thought how corny he sounded. Like a real jerk. If *she* were one of those girls, she would tell him to take a hike.

"Hey, go soak your head, guy," one of the girls called out, and the others laughed between breaths.

Jenny put her hand over her mouth to keep from laughing, too.

"What're you laughing at, Friedman?" Terry asked absently, while his eyes still followed the girls as they jogged ahead of the station wagon.

"You."

"You're looking at Amusements Unlimited." Terry shook his shaggy head.

"You went out with Janie Messler, didn't you?" Jenny asked suddenly.

Terry shrugged. "She thinks I'm a monster."

"It didn't last?"

"Hey, I don't know what went wrong, okay?" Terry pulled on the brim of his sun visor, still watching the girls ahead of them.

"Hey, Terry, watch out!" Jenny cried.

Crunch — it was too late. Terry stamped on the brakes, backending the car in front as it stopped for a light.

"Friedman? You still there?" Terry sat

there with his eyes shut. Jenny suspected he'd scared himself.

"Right here. On the edge of the seat. Pinned on the edge of hysteria. I could've become a statistic," Jenny said.

"My father's gonna kill me." Terry looked glum.

The girls turned around and shook their heads, laughing at him. The driver of the car in front got out to inspect the damage.

"I'm so sorry, Terry," Jenny said sympathetically.

"Hey, man, that's the breaks," he said, getting out of the car. Jenny followed him. The front bumper was caved in, a perfect V. The twisted chrome winked at them, almost a taunt. Terry clapped his hand over his forehead.

"What will your father say?" Jenny asked.

"Oh, nothing," Terry said flatly. "He'll just quietly hang me by my thumbs until I'm dead."

"You seem to be taking this well," Jenny said. She knew that she would've been very upset. Her mother would've been furious, and she would've felt like an idiot. Terry seemed cool.

"Hey, what's done is done, you know? I blew it." He shrugged.

The next hour was spent exchanging phone numbers and insurance company information, and waiting for the police to arrive.

Terry and Jenny sat in the car, making

jokes and goofing around to pass the time.

"I can just see the headlines: TEEN DRIVES HIMSELF AND FRIEND TO EARLY DEATH BECAUSE OF ROADSIDE ATTRACTIONS." Terry chuckled.

"Roadside *dis*tractions," amended Jenny. Josh would say that, she decided. "It's a little long for a headline, but it has a nice ring."

Terry beat his fist against the steering wheel. "Just why did I get so distracted by those girls? I mean, how stupid can you get? They obviously weren't interested."

"I think you were legally blind at the time," Jenny suggested.

"*Lust*fully blind is more like it," Terry corrected his friend.

Jenny whistled, thinking that this was an odd conversation. There were times when she was with girls who would be so entranced by a cute boy they would nearly forget they were driving. But still, with Terry, it seemed different somehow. He was not merely distracted — he was consumed. "I know what you're going through," she said.

"No you don't, Friedman. You've got a girl friend."

"Does that make a difference?" Jenny asked in surprise.

"Yeah, you have a love life. For me, things are as dry as the Sahara," Terry replied.

"*I* have a love life?" Did Terry know something she didn't know? Jenny imagined Josh bragging like some boys — he wouldn't do that, would he? She thought she knew him pretty well, but now she was beginning to find out that maybe that wasn't true, so he fabricated stories about the two of them. After all, Terry was his best friend. Best friends share everything, don't they?

"What makes you think I have a love life? Have I told you I do?" Jenny asked pointedly.

"Well, no. We've never talked about it before. I just figured. . . ." Terry scratched his head.

"You figured wrong." Jenny was relieved that it was all in Terry's mind. "And anyway, sex isn't everything."

"That's easy to say," said Terry.

"Girls don't think about it all the time," Jenny said. "They also like to talk, and be friends, and have other interests, just like you do."

Terry turned to his friend, looking puzzled. "You know, Janie said something like that once. 'Can't you think of anything else?' she said. She also said I was acting like a monster. She said it was like being with an octopus. I told her I was listening to what she was saying. But you know, it was really hard to concentrate. Because I wanted to talk, but I also wanted to touch."

Terry looked vaguely uncomfortable. "You know, Friedman, to tell you the truth, if one of those girls by the road was interested, I'd clam up. Or say something stupid and turn her off. I can't figure myself out."

"Don't torture yourself over it, Terry," Jenny tried to comfort him.

"Well, I'm telling you, but nobody else. You know how guys talk about girls. I don't want to look like a big failure," Terry confessed.

"You don't look like a failure to me," Jenny said. "Anyway, a lot of guys are all talk."

"Yeah, maybe." Then he fixed his attention on the revolving red beacon of the approaching police car. "Hey, there's a cop. I'd better get out and show him my driver's license."

Terry got out of the car and the conversation ended. Jenny sat and watched while the police officer wrote down all the information he needed.

Jenny had been surprised when Terry admitted that he wasn't very sure of himself around girls. That powerhouse routine was just an act. Could it be that boys were as nervous as girls?

There seemed to be some unspoken rules to being male. Sympathy, for example, was not part of their unwritten code. Yet there was a certain comradery among the boys. They liked each other, didn't they, in spite of the competition? They liked to feel they could do anything, without help from anyone. Except as part of a team, where they were allowed to join forces and be something greater than their individual selves.

When she had been little, she had often thought about what it would be like to be a boy, to have what appeared to be a special freedom. Boys had seemed independent and secretive. She'd thought they were never afraid of anything. Even her little brother Bernie had hardly ever cried. What Terry had told her was probably the most she would hear about a boy's secret thoughts. He had brought her a little closer to understanding boys better, yet she was still sorry that they weren't more open.

Terry climbed back in the car, and placed a ticket on the dashboard. "Well, I guess surfing's out now."

The sun was disappearing behind a copse of eucalyptus trees.

"Oh, I don't know. How's your night vision?" Jenny joked.

"Funny, Friedman. Let's go home. I'm not into feeling my way through the ocean today."

Jenny laughed. The whole scene — waiting for the police to come because Terry was distracted by three girls — seemed very funny now. She thought of all the trouble girls and boys got themselves into chasing after each other. But why then, if there was this great magnetism between the sexes, was there also this major misunderstanding over what boys and girls wanted?

"Sorry, man," Terry said, when Josh took his board out of the back of the station wagon.

"Hey, it's okay. Just promise me something. Keep your eyes on the road."

Terry held up two fingers in a peace sign, nodded soberly, then tore off in an impressive cloud of dust.

Chapter 11

Josh was dreaming that he had washed up on a desert island and a group of girls were surrounding him. They were wearing long caftan-like dresses. It was the kind of dream he liked having. The air was perfumed with flowers, the sun haloed the girls' heads, and he squinted into their smiling faces. Then their faces divided into segments as though he were viewing them through a kaleidoscope.

But in reality, Cathy and Elyse were having a pillow fight, and one of the pillows had landed on Josh's face. Cathy had knocked over a bottle of cologne, which accounted for the scent. The morning sun streamed in through the gauzy curtains of Elyse's living room. There was a reason for everything.

Everything, that is, except why he and Jenny had not changed back into themselves. Josh realized the fairy godfather had forgotten them, and his spirits sank with the thought.

He got dressed quickly, filled with the

dawning knowledge that he had expected to be playing baseball today.

"We're going to the mall," Elyse said. There was a major discussion going on about clothes now, and jeans and T-shirts were scattered everywhere. The girls were slipping in and out of clothes and sharing make-up. Josh felt as though he were viewing some kind of tribal rite. He was mesmerized by the sight.

"I have to go," he said quickly. "I have a dress rehearsal today."

"If we were as dedicated as you, Jenny, we wouldn't spend so much money," Cathy said as she packed her things.

Connie was on the telephone to her boyfriend. The other girls finished dressing and threw pillows at her to get her attention. "Okay, okay. I'll get off," Connie yelled.

"She and Randy are joined at the ear," Cathy said.

Finally, everyone piled into Elyse's car and they dropped Josh at Jenny's house. "Will you be at the baseball game later?" someone asked.

The thought of missing the game stung Josh, but he managed, "It depends on what time rehearsal ends."

Fear splashed over Josh as he watched the girls drive off. He would have to dance, unless that jerky fairy godfather appeared soon. He absolutely couldn't! Sure, he was sort of getting the hang of ballet — the "hang" of it was right. He was just hanging in there.

He strode into the house, planning what to do next. It was inexcusable of the godfather not to keep his end of the bargain. Surely he wouldn't make them go through this! Josh would have to dance in Jenny's dress rehearsal, and the game — cripes, she would have to play ball for him!

He called her the minute he got home.

"Hi. How am I doing?" he asked.

"You're doing fine. How am I?" Suddenly, Jenny sounded worried. "Josh, what's happened to our fairy godfather? Weren't we supposed to wake up as ourselves?"

"I thought that was the general idea," Josh agreed.

"I kind of planned to be me for my dress rehearsal," Jenny waited.

"It's been on my mind, too. Look, I'll do what I can, okay?" Josh said, hoping he sounded confident.

He hung up and rushed into the den, being careful to close the door behind him. He turned the computer on, inserted a diskette, and waited. Counting the minutes, staring at the screen. Then squeezing his eyes shut and envisioning the change. What would it feel like? He hadn't been conscious of the first change. Was there any way they could make the second change happen? Surely their combined hysteria was a force to be reckoned with. Couldn't they maybe move molecules just by thinking really hard?

Nothing happened. Josh swallowed hard.

He had really thought the fairy godfather would change them back, even though he hadn't shown his face since that first day. No promises had been made, but it seemed impossible that he would keep them in body bondage for more than three days. What possible good was being done keeping them trapped in each other's bodies?

Finally, Josh despaired of staring at the computer screen. No use fussing over it, he decided. It was a quarter to ten, and he had to prepare for Jenny's rehearsal. He changed into Jenny's leotard and began to warm up.

The doorbell rang. It was Jenny.

"I couldn't bear the suspense. I had to see for myself." She strode ahead of Josh into the den.

"Sorry to disappoint you, but he's not showing up. He's very shy."

"Or a liar." She stared at the computer screen. "Haven't you made your point, Fairy Godfather?" she demanded.

Silence followed. Josh brushed against her. "Maybe we have more to learn," he suggested hopefully.

She glanced around the den, then touched things — the paperweight, books, pencils. "It's only been a few days, but I miss this place."

"Yeah, I know what you mean. What are we gonna do, Jen?"

Their eyes met. Josh experienced a flood of longing for the way things used to be, just three days before.

Jenny was the first to speak. "I guess we go through with it, then. You'll have to dance; I'll play your game."

Josh and Jenny held hands, not speaking for a while. "The slumber party was a character-building experience," he teased.

"Did you learn anything?" Jenny asked, smiling.

"Sure. I know where they're going to college, what they're wearing to the mall, and all about their sex lives. How's that?" He grinned triumphantly.

"Josh!"

"I thought that was pretty impressive. How about you?"

"I was going surfing with your friend Terry, but we had a small accident. . . ." She told him the disastrous story.

"Terry had a bruised nose once because he didn't look where he was going and ran into a door. He was looking at a girl," Josh told her.

"I can see he has a long history of this kind of thing," said Jenny. "But you know, at first I thought he was a jerk, then I discovered that he's the most open of your friends."

"Hey, tell me about openness. Your friends are really into gut-spilling," he complained. "We're going to learn all each other's secrets."

"All the better to know you with, my dear," Jenny giggled.

* * *

Josh felt like Peter Pan, or maybe Wendy, outfitted in the white leotard, tutu, and tights.

The studio was in chaos. He stood apart from the others, watching while Mrs. Herbert sewed elastic on one girl's pointe shoes and then proceeded to wipe a grubby mark off another's leotard. Two girls crowded in front of a small mirror in the restroom, applying their makeup.

Josh had put on Jenny's makeup at home because he didn't want to have to do it in public. It was fun, like an art project, he decided. He thought he made Jenny look pretty good.

However, Mrs. Herbert was critical. "You don't have enough makeup on, Jenny. Here, let me help you."

Mrs. Herbert had a pair of hands that would do better with a piece of sandpaper on wood than tissue on skin. If Mrs. Herbert had any children, Josh reflected, he pitied them a diaper change.

"Feels like a layer of my skin's being removed," Josh commented.

"Nonsense, Jennifer," Mrs. Herbert remarked tartly. "The skin needs a little stimulation, more color enhancement."

"Yeah, right," answered Josh, squinting.

Finally, Mrs. Herbert bustled off to help someone else, and Jessica came up to Josh. "Jenny, you look great. Can I do your hair?"

He looked around and noticed the other girls were doing each other's hair. "Sure, thanks," he said gratefully. He had seen Jenny twist it into a thick coil for her performances but he hadn't quite figured out how to do it himself.

Then there were the new pointe shoes. Josh had been instructed by Jenny to sew ribbons and elastic on them, cut out the satin toe, pull out the insole, step on them, bend the shank in half, and beat them against a wall. All this to make them wearable!

He still thought it was a weird feeling standing on pointe, even if they were not his own toes he was balancing on. It was abnormal to stand on one's toes like that, he decided. He remembered Jenny telling him about her first pair of toe shoes, and how excited she'd been to get them.

Everyone lined up to do preperformance warm-ups. Josh had them down pretty well. The practicing had paid off. He felt more in control, better balanced. Fine-tuned. Not to mention completely terrified.

"It's time," Jessica announced in a hushed whisper, placing her fingers on Jenny's arm. All the dancers lined up in their white leotards and tutus, ready and waiting behind the curtains which divided the dressing room from the studio. Josh stood in the shadows, next to Jessica, thinking of how Jenny would perform. Think Jenny, he told himself, closing his eyes, conjuring up the image of her dancing lightly across a stage.

The music of Chopin began, slowly, notes dropping into the silence like raindrops as the dancers twirled out from the dressing room into the studio room. Josh followed Jessica, charting her movements. She spun quickly across the studio, no sooner leaving one complete turn than whirling into another. The music of the next dance began lightly, moving into a gentle, but joyous, waltz. All eyes were on Jenny now. Panic flooded Josh, but he pushed through it before it could weigh him down. He thought of Jenny: her effort, her grace, the concentration that went into her dancing. He moved forward, determined to do it right.

Exuberantly, he waltzed across the stage, Jenny's arms arched gracefully around him, then he spun at the end with palms outstretched, neck curved back. He had no idea how he looked, yet he could tell by the way the movements felt that it was coming together. Excitement trembled inside him as he danced, but he pressed it back down, concentrating hard on his image of Jenny.

Mrs. Herbert frowned and leaned close to Madame Craft, who was another teacher at the school. A heavyset woman next to them inclined her ear to the pair's conversation. She might be someone from the ballet school Jenny wanted to go to, Josh thought nervously. They kept looking at Jenny while they talked. He knew they were talking about her. Would Jenny be disqualified from auditioning if her performance wasn't up to par? He pushed that thought from his mind and turned his attention to the other dancers, who formed a half-moon behind him, their arms moving like wings, in unison.

Josh recalled the way Jenny always walked around touching things. It was something he'd forgotten about her until he'd noticed her doing the same thing while she was in his body. She was in touch with her senses — as though there was comfort to be drawn from the texture of objects, the shape of things. Maybe it was a uniquely female trait, though he didn't know for sure. Regardless, touch, sight, and sound were also part of Jenny's approach to dance. Sometimes she looked as though she had an intimate relationship with the air itself. Josh thought of this as he let the music fill him until he brimmed with its rhythm. Then he took a deep breath, envisioned what Jenny would look like, and plunged ahead.

The next dance was bolder, more open and free. He bounded diagonally across the studio, executing grand *jetés*, whirling into a turn, arms flung forward, then back behind him, head arched over Jenny's chest. Breath coming and going, air sifting through her fingers, toe shoes thudding against the wood floor, a blur of faces as he spun and jumped. Jenny's body carried him, almost effortlessly, lightly, as though he was a feather being lifted by a strong and powerful wind. That was it, he thought excitedly. That was the right feeling, it was happening, he was really dancing — dancing well. He liked the feeling and rode it eagerly to its ending, reveling in the strange sensation of twirling on his toes.

Feeling strangely confident, Josh finished the dance with a new, unexpected turn. His knees bent outward at a new angle, arms suspended on either side like a pair of graceful wings. A flurry of gasps escaped from some of the other dancers.

Oh, no, he thought, I blew it. Despair crept over him as he saw Mrs. Herbert moving purposefully towards him.

"Jennifer, that was superb. I must say, you've created something different. A little unusual, but interesting. I'm very excited. How did you do that? Can you repeat it?"

Josh stared at her in astonishment. She was serious? She was! He had created something new in the world of dance. How incredible!

"I think what you've just done is quite innovative and wonderful," Mrs. Herbert exclaimed, and Josh got the distinct impression that Mrs. Herbert didn't get excited all that often.

"You're kidding! Hey, man, that's great!" Josh declared, shaking Mrs. Herbert's hand vigorously. He didn't know exactly what he'd done that was so wonderful, but flattery could get him just about anywhere — in anyone's body!

"Jennifer, please," Mrs. Herbert became stiff and uncomfortable at the unexpected gesture from her pupil.

"Sorry." Josh took a couple of steps backward. Behind him, Jessica giggled. "Hey, what does this mean? Do you think I'll be accepted into the school?" Josh asked.

"As I've said before, you have an excellent chance." Mrs. Herbert's answer was curt and honest. "And you are certainly ready for your audition."

Nothing definite, but still. . . . Wait until I tell Jenny what happened, he thought excitedly.

Chapter 12

Gary Krupp saw Josh and waved to him from the pitcher's mound. "Hey, Friedman, get over here!"

Jenny had been watching the other players warm up, trying to visualize how she would play now, when it mattered so much. This was an important game to the Druids. Obediently, she ran over to where Gary stood.

"Why don't you try hitting a few. Maybe you'll do better today." Coach Jacobs looked hopefully at Jenny.

"Yeah, sure." Jenny walked over to home plate and picked up a bat. It was a heavier one than she would usually choose, but then she was Josh, not Jenny. Keep it in mind, she told herself, you're Josh, not Jenny. Be him, be him, be him. . . .

Gary pitched a ball. Jenny hit it. It traveled in a straight line back to him.

"Hey, good one." Gary grinned.

Jenny knew he was being sarcastic, but

she didn't care. They were all watching Josh, waiting to see what he could do. The anticipation weighed on her, and she likened it to the feeling she got when beginning a dance.

Jenny smacked another ball into mid-field and the others cheered. The Rams from Ryder High School arrived and practice ended. The Druids took their positions in the field, and the cheerleaders gathered along the sideline. A sparse audience filled the two bottom rows of the bleachers.

In the past few months, Jenny had rarely made it to Josh's games, simply because her own schedule really didn't allow it. She wished she could have been more supportive of him, knowing how important an audience was to any performer.

The game began. Jenny took Josh's place at first base. The first batter whacked the ball straight to first, right into Jenny's mitt. She tagged the player.

"One out!" shouted the referee. The whole team looked approvingly at Josh.

The next batter his a fly ball, which Gary caught.

"Two out!" the referee cried.

The momentum gathered. The next batter struck out, sending the Druids up to bat.

Relieved to find she was not in the first inning's batting order, Jenny sat back to enjoy the game.

The Druids did badly — two strikeouts and one player on first base, then a fly ball put them back out in the field. Jenny managed to handle everything that came to first base, but still the team was losing. The Rams made two runs to the Druids' none in seven innings.

In the eighth inning, Josh was up to bat. Jenny was petrified. She tried to think of Josh, of dancing, of everything she knew all at once. Her mind blurred with the confusion of it all, then she shook free of it, closed her eyes, and willed herself to concentrate.

Crouched over the plate, she concentrated hard on the ball as it arced toward her. She swung hard and missed. "Strike one!" Taunts rose from the outfield, but she closed them out. With her full force, she swung again. Whack! The ball bounced into center field. Jenny loped to first base. The batter behind her struck out, putting the Druids in the field once more.

"We've only got one more inning to deliver ourselves, boys, now let's get to it!" yelled Coach Jacobs. He was mad, and his face turned ruddy as he glowered at the other team.

Jenny scooped up a foul ball and tossed it to Gary. One out. Come on, Druids, sock it to 'em, she thought, shoving her fist into the warm curve of the mitt.

The next batter hit a high ball, which landed in center field. With someone on base, the team got highly nervous. Another batter sent the ball right into Gary's hand, and he tagged the lone base runner out.

The Druids were up to bat. The first two batters struck out, then the next three got on base. The bases were loaded. Jenny was up next.

"It all depends on you, Friedman," the coach said gruffly. "Get on base and bring these boys home."

Jenny nodded. The responsibility of having a performance depend on her was familiar. Slowly, Jenny moved toward home plate, thinking about what Josh would do in the same situation. Then she thought about dance, of grace, of the fluid motion of the bat moving to meet the ball. To that she must add force to get the ball really out there. She had to use every resource — the best of her and Josh — put it all together, make it work!

Fear began to worm its way around her resolve, but she pressed it down, concentrating, every fiber tuned to what was happening.

The ball curved toward her. She swung. Crack! The ball soared high in the air, arcing over the diamond.

"Run!" screamed voices from behind, and Jeremy obeyed, streaking out toward first, then following hot on the heels of the other three teammates. Sean Cunningham made it home, then Gary Grupp, then Eddie Collander. The wind whistled through Josh's thin gray jersey, causing it to flap around her. Jenny felt the power of Josh's body propelling her forward, his legs like thick pistons beneath her, and she liked it. She turned to see the outfielder pick up the ball and hurl it toward the pitcher. He missed it. Jenny turned on the steam and sped forward, leaping onto third base, and finally, she slid across home plate.

A grand slam. Screams enveloped her. She got up and dusted herself off, while the coach and team members gathered round, hugging her, slapping her on the back. This time, she didn't recoil from the gestures. They even felt good.

"Score's four to two now," Gary Krupp said. "No need to worry, the Druids have the game, thanks to you, Josh."

"Friedman, that was fantastic! Man, you saved us," Coach Jacobs said. And coming from him, even Jenny knew that was some compliment.

But she didn't need the coach's, or anybody else's, approval. She knew that she'd done a fine job. Josh's mom waved from the bleachers, and Jenny waved back. This time, when it really mattered, she had done what Josh would've done.

One of the boys came over and hugged Jenny. "Hey, Josh, you were great. You're coming to Shawn's, aren't you? We're celebrating."

"Oh, sure."

After the game there was always a gathering at Shawn's Soda Shop. Jenny knew Josh looked forward to those times with the guys.

Pushed toward the locker room by the flow of activity, Jenny breathed dust, sweat, and exuberance. Fortunately, everyone was so intent on getting into the showers that Josh was ignored. Jenny ducked out, electing to meet the others at Shawn's.

Later, at the soda shop, boys crammed up against the counter, ordering soft drinks, talking, and joking.

"An impressive grand slam, Friedman," Eddie said. Slap on the shoulder again. Smiles of jubilation. The guys were rough-and-tumble out on the field, but they were almost affectionate with one another now. Funny, boys hardly touched each other, except when they had something to celebrate and share. The small soda shop shimmered with excitement and glowing, triumphant faces. Jenny felt pleased to be a part of it.

"Yeah, never thought you had it in you," grinned Gary Krupp.

"Five to two — can you believe it? We didn't need Eddie's run, but we got it anyway," Sean beamed.

"Hey, man, we're victorious," Doug Kallinsky emphasized.

Jenny took a good look at Doug. She knew him only as Cathy's boyfriend. He seemed nice enough, but why had they broken up? Josh had never told her the reason.

"Let's drink to victory!" Terry Fields shouted. Everyone raised their Cokes.

"Hurray, Druids!" they chorused. "Hurray, Josh!"

Glasses chimed. Jenny thought of her own parties with her friends and how different they were. We would talk about victory, too, she reflected. We are competitive, but not quite so adversarial about it. And there are so many other things we talk about. Somehow, there are not as many off-limits subjects for girls as there are for guys.

Jenny shouldered her way through the room, listening to the boys.

"I've never hit so well in my entire life, except for that game back in April. Remember, Gary?" Sean asked.

"Yeah, I remember. We beat the Royals eight to one," replied Gary.

"Hey, Burgerface, you working today?" Sean cried.

Jenny turned around to see who bore the title Burgerface. Of course, Eddie Collander, who worked at Burger King.

"Later today. Why?" asked Eddie.

"How about giving me a free meal?" Sean replied.

"You want to get me fired?"

"I thought you were the manager now."

"He's head French fry chef," someone else put in.

"Grease city," another boy offered. "Bending over those greasy fries all day."

Jenny knew this was their ritual — insults, jabs, and jokes. After a brief silence, they started right up again, but she found herself on the outside, looking in. Girls wouldn't say things like that. They tease, but usually it's more gentle, and they generally try to make each other feel good about themselves.

The conversation shifted to Saturday night plans and slowly, the group began to disband. More back-patting, bear-hugging, shouted farewells. A couple of boys wrestled playfully near the door, and others casually pushed past them. Jenny stared at the empty glasses lined up on the counter, the jackets being pulled on, the jukebox, suddenly quiet. She finally walked out with Terry Fields.

"I want you to know, Friedman, I talked to Janie again," Terry said in a low voice.

"Good. What did she say?" Jenny asked.

"We're going out. I told her I had turned over a new leaf." He smiled.

"You're not such a rotten guy after all?" she joked.

"That's what I told her. I promised not to throw myself at her anymore."

Jenny laughed. "Good luck," she called as she said good-bye to Terry, the brief flare of intimacy warming her as she walked away.

Chapter 13

"How'd it go?"

The question was posed in unison. Jenny and Josh both laughed and linked hands. They were in Josh's backyard.

"You hit a grand slam, and won the game," Jenny said.

"Hey, good work!" He hugged her fiercely. "You did great, too. Mrs. Herbert says you've created something new in the world of dance."

"You're kidding? That's unbelievable!" Jenny cried.

"I thought so, too. Especially since I wouldn't know how to do it again if I tried."

Jenny was thoughtful. "So I guess if we were to be stuck this way forever, we could manage."

"I guess so, but being you is tough. I never realized how hard you worked at dancing," admitted Josh. "I didn't know how caught up you were in it, what it meant to you. I mean, now that I know what it feels like to be you dancing, I can understand. Its great! Before, I guess I was jealous because it took time away from us. I figured you didn't care enough about me."

"And now?"

"I know that's not true. You have to be dedicated to be the talented ballerina that you are. It's something that you have to do. I didn't take that seriously before."

Jenny plucked a few blades of grass and braided them togther. "I always thought you weren't serious enough about anything — before I was you. When I played baseball, I realized how important it was to you, even though you're always pretty casual about it. I guess I did the same thing — didn't take you seriously, that is. I learned a lot from your friends, too."

"Yeah, I learned a lot from your friends, Jenny." Josh agreed. "They sure talk about boys a lot. They're always trying to figure them out. I'll bet most boys don't know there's that much to say about themselves. I think it's nice, and it shows how much girls care about their relationships — not just boy-girl relationships, either." He stopped, then added, "But I wonder how much you've told your friends about me. And why don't they talk to boys the way they talk to each other?"

Jenny frowned at the last question. Why don't they? "Maybe it's because they don't get the same kind of response from boys as they do from each other. Maybe they're scared."

Suddenly, she was remembering something she'd forgotten. Something that had happened back when she and Josh were first going out together. She had been so wild about him she could barely see straight, and she'd been grateful for the imposed discipline of dance to keep her balance. But one night when they had been walking along the beach, she had told him she loved him.

He hadn't replied. He hadn't called her for a week. She had become frightened that she had scared him off, just by expressing her feelings. Was love too terrifying an announcement?

"I don't remember it," Josh said, when Jenny brought it up to him now.

"You must!" she cried, horrified that he could forget a major incident over which she had agonized. She had even taken the problem to Elyse because she had really needed someone to talk to.

"Well, maybe I do," he offered grudgingly.

"What did you think then?"

He shrugged. "I had to think about what you said. It sounded heavy. Nobody had ever said that to me before, except my parents. I'd never loved a girl before, and what if I didn't love you? We hadn't known each other very long. It seemed to be happening too fast. I had to be sure."

"But you didn't talk to me for a week," Jenny reminded him. "I thought you were gone."

"It wasn't that long, was it?"

"Yes, it was exactly seven days. Then you called me as though nothing had happened," she recalled.

"Nothing *had* happened," Josh insisted.

Jenny sighed. "When did you first know you loved me?"

"A couple of months ago when we were sitting in a restaurant and you were talking seriously about something, with a big blob of mustard on your nose," Josh said sincerely, and smiled.

"Really? Why didn't you tell me?" asked Jenny.

"I was too busy laughing."

"You goon," she said in pretended disgust. "Didn't you think I would have liked to have known that little piece of information?"

"I didn't think it was that important to you. You already knew, anyway, didn't you?" Josh asked.

"No, I didn't know. I'm not a mind reader, Josh. I can't believe you didn't think it was important."

He shrugged. "Sorry."

"It just goes to show you, when I was thinking about romance and love, you weren't there yet."

"And you haven't been thinking about other things when I have," Josh added.

Jenny frowned. "I've been thinking about 'other things.' I think about how nice it would be to be that close. But also, I know I have to be ready, and that right now I'm not. So you're way ahead of me."

"I think girls must feel more vulnerable than guys," Josh said feelingly. "Like I've felt in your body sometimes. But I'm impatient," Josh said. "Do you think we'll ever want the same thing at the same time?"

"Who knows? But I guess it helps to know what each other is feeling. And that we aren't always going to feel the same way at the same time."

"Seems like the lines of communication have been out of order for awhile," he commented.

"Yeah. Let's get a repairman on them right away," Jenny quipped.

"That's a Josh comment if ever I heard one." He laughed. "Are you taking over my identity, too? This is beginning to sound even more like the *Twilight Zone*."

"If we really want to spook ourselves, we can freak out over the fact that we have no idea when this is going to end." Jenny stretched out on the grass.

Josh lay down beside her. "Okay, close your eyes and make a wish. I'm doing the same thing at the same time, see?" he teased.

"I don't see too well with my eyes closed, silly."

"Of course, I won't ask you what your wish is, because that's bad luck." Josh explained. "But maybe if we wish at the same time, it will have more power."

"You're getting really superstitious."

Josh didn't answer. They lay there for five minutes, wishing intensely. Then Jenny propped herself on Josh's elbows to view the two of them. "No visible change."

"Follow me," he ordered. They got up and made their way through Josh's house to a hall closet. Josh pulled down a dust-laden Ouija board and blew off the dust.

"I haven't done this in years," Jenny exclaimed. They set the board up on the patio table.

She went first, placing Josh's fingertips lightly on the planchette. "Oh, Ouija, when will Josh Friedman and I change places?"

"I don't think you need to be so formal," Josh whispered.

The planchette made circular motions across the board, settling on the N in the alphabet. Jenny tensed. "Shhh! We're getting somewhere!"

Then it moved quickly to E, made a beeline for V, then moved back to E. Slowly, the planchette came to rest on the R.

"N-E-V E-R," Jenny and Josh spelled it simultaneously. "Never." They repeated the word several times, until it seemed to lose its meaning.

"Maybe 'never' means something good in a foreign language," suggested Josh.

"Do you mean 'never' like 'not ever,' oh, Ouija?" Jenny asked timidly.

The planchette moved once more to reply — Y-E-S.

"Here, let me try." Jenny moved aside so that Josh could place Jenny's fingers on the planchette. "Ouija, what are you saying to

me? Are you saying that I will never be myself again?"

Y-E-S.

"It's not true!" Josh cried in horror.

Then came the Ouija's ominous reply —
Y-E-S, I-T I-S T-R-U-E.

Jenny burst into tears.

Chapter 14

Sunday morning, Josh awakened in his own room. In his own body. He had been prepared, yet not prepared, to be Jenny forever. After that business with the Ouija board, and the heavy possibility of never being himself again, he was incredibly relieved.

He stared down at himself and felt immense joy. This body was all his — total Josh Friedman. He looked again, thinking, yes, it's me. Welcome home, me! We should have some kind of celebration — but there was only the soft stirring of the wind outside the window, and down the hall the murmur of a radio playing, but no sounding cymbals. No brass band. Because no one except he and Jenny knew the truth.

He got up and stood in front of the full-length mirror, naked. There was no telling when you were dealing with unexplained computer beings, what might happen.

But the tall, lanky frame was all there. Seal-brown hair, green eyes, and a grin that he had missed. He was the same guy, only he had been through a few heavy changes. He knew something most guys his age didn't know. Or most guys any age, for that matter. He knew what it was really like to be a girl. A very special girl.

Right now, he wanted to get on the phone to Jenny. No, he wanted to *see* Jenny, as herself. His longing for her was strong, but there was something else. A sense of connectedness, knowing that they shared something no one else had.

Josh slid into a pair of jeans and combed his hair, noting that Jenny had used some new kind of herbal-scented shampoo. He liked it. It was like she had left her memory on his body.

His room was really clean, too — books all stacked neatly on his desk, no clothes on the floor, everything hung up. Nice.

He breezed into the kitchen, possessed by serious hunger. "Hiya, Mom," he greeted his mother with a quick peck on the cheek.

"Hi, dear." She watched as he ripped two bananas from the bunch and shoved them into the blender, along with a couple of heaping teaspoons of protein powder, wheat germ, milk, and two eggs. Then he set the blender on high.

"Hungry, Josh?" she inquired, the corners of her mouth turning up in amusement.

"Yeah. You don't have to worry about my appetite," he declared, pouring the thick liquid into a tall glass. Of course, he knew she didn't understand the change in him, and never would. She would pass it off as an adolescent stage. Josh was suddenly grateful for the preconceived notions of parents — they sure saved him a lot of explanation.

At approximately the same time, Jenny Knudson began to yawn. As she climbed up through the cottony layers of sleep, she realized something was different. She opened her eyes in her own bedroom.

She gasped with pure delight, relief, and a feeling so good she didn't know what to call it. It was a little like the soaring sensation she got when a dance was going well.

She pulled back the covers to look at herself. Sure enough, she *was* herself. Restored at last!

She smoothed her fingers along her face, closed her eyes, and opened them again. The feeling was wonderful. Her body was like a long lost friend, and she scrambled out of bed onto the soft carpet to do a series of *pliés*. Then she did a series of effortless turns, reveling in the movements — swift, light, easy. The feeling was joyous — she felt like yelling, "Hey, I'm whole!" She arched her back and did a flip, her hair grazing the carpet. The sun slanted through the triangular window, catching its golden highlights.

Her alarm went off then. Jenny spun and stretched until she decided to get dressed. And there was her whole wardrobe, which she had really missed. She picked out her favorite jeans, and a purple T-shirt, covering it with the hand-painted sweat shirt Josh had chosen to wear the other day. Her own clothes, her own shoes felt so good. "Walking in my own shoes again," she sang to herself on the way down to breakfast.

"Hi, Mom, hi, Bernie!" she called gaily, skipping across the dining area to the kitchen.

"Well, hi, yourself," her mother looked up from the paper, her eyebrows arched in surprise. "To what do we owe this burst of enthusiasm?"

"To rediscovery," Jenny held up a glass of orange juice in a gesture of a toast.

"Oh, yeah?" Bernie pushed his glasses higher onto his nose, viewing his sister with interest.

"Yes." She got out her cereal and shook some into a bowl. But she couldn't tell her family that she had just rediscovered herself, after a journey as Josh Friedman. And now, feeling confident that no one would ever know otherwise, she felt like being incredibly mysterious about it all.

Just as Jenny scooped the last of her cereal from the bowl, the doorbell rang. It was Josh, grinning wide. Jenny stood on tiptoe to kiss him.

He held her for a brief moment, then took her hand. "Boy, does that ever feel good," he said. Then he lowered his voice, "Do you think we can find that fairy godfather now?"

"Well, I sure hope so. He ought to make

an appearance. I think he owes us an explanation."

Josh said hi to Bernie and Mrs. Knudson, then Jenny led the way to the den. She turned on the computer and put in a diskette.

In a few moments, they both heard a voice. "Aha, I expected you would both check in. How are you feeling out there?"

The nearly forgotten, roughly hewn features of the fairy godfather came into full view, and he held up his hand with the unbroken lifeline.

"So there you are!" Jenny exclaimed, leaning over the keyboard. "We're feeling just fine, now, thank you very much. What happened to you? Why didn't you show up earlier?"

"I was detained elsewhere — another appointment. Sorry, I had trouble getting here. Traffic, you know."

"Why did you do this to us?" Josh blurted out.

"I seem to remember you wanted it — you wanted desperately to understand each other."

"There must've been an easier way," Jenny said.

"Maybe," the fairy godfather started slowly, "but in no other way would you have reached the point of merge. You sat on the brink of becoming, truly becoming someone else — of the opposite gender. You stood in another person's shoes, you made the decisions that person had to make, you lived for that person. Plainly speaking, I daresay you know each other inside, as well as outside now."

Josh and Jenny looked at each other. The joy and relief at seeing each other normal again was enough to make them not care how or why it had happened, only that they were safe again, and together.

"Yes, we do," Jenny responded. "But we still don't know who you are and why you did this in the first place."

"Oh, you are such a questioning lot sometimes, aren't you?"

The fairy godfather smiled gently, compassionately, as though he knew the depths of everything they might be thinking. "I am here to grant wishes, impossible wishes they may seem, but they are of the nonmaterial variety you have just experienced." He was quiet, offering no more than that.

"But where are you from? What are you?" Josh persisted.

The fairy godfather smiled, then his image began to fade off the screen. Jenny reached out to touch it, pressing her palms against the glass, but he was gone by then. The den was silent.

Finally, Jenny spoke. "What really happened to us, Josh?"

"I guess we'll never know completely," he said reaching for her hand. "But we're safe now. Ourselves. No more wishes, okay?"

"I'm not even going to *wonder*," Jenny said, shaking her head. "Hey, the Ouija board was wrong."

He shrugged at this, even though yesterday the Ouija's message had doomed them both. "How can you believe in a board and a piece of plastic?"

"For three days, we've believed in a fairy godfather that nobody else has seen. I think that's comparatively weird."

"True. So now what? Where were we three days ago, before we were so rudely interrupted?"

"We were arguing about sex and love, ballet and baseball."

"I think we can pick up where we left off," Josh said.

"Except we're not arguing now. Maybe we understand each other a little better," Jenny smiled. "I feel so close to you."

"Hey, likewise, Jen." He grinned, slipped his hands under her arms and drew her closer. "If we could live through this experience, we can handle anything together. We're a team."

"There's a little bit of you in the way I think now," she said. "It helps."

"Same here. I also think I now have extrasensory perception where you're concerned," Josh said.

"Oh, really?"

Josh kissed her. Jenny closed her eyes and let her thoughts spiral, concentrating on the kiss. A curious, weightless sensation spread through her limbs, and she let herself be lifted and carried by it, deliciously feather-light.

"See what I mean?" Josh said, kissing her between words.

"No," answered Jenny, confused.

"I could tell that you wanted to kiss me, without your even saying a word." He grinned down at her, threading his fingers through her hair.

"Really?" she whispered, smiling.

They kissed again, pressed against one another, the green light from the computer screen shimmering behind them.

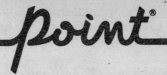

Other books you will enjoy,
about real kids like you!

☐	42365-7	**Blind Date** R.L. Stine	$2.50
☐	41248-5	**Double Trouble** Barthe DeClements and Christopher Greimes	$2.75
☐	41432-1	**Just a Summer Romance** Ann M. Martin	$2.50
☐	40935-2	**Last Dance** Caroline B. Cooney	$2.50
☐	41549-2	**The Lifeguard** Richie Tankersley Cusack	$2.50
☐	33829-3	**Life Without Friends** Ellen Emerson White	$2.75
☐	40548-9	**A Royal Pain** Ellen Conford	$2.50
☐	41823-8	**Simon Pure** Julian F. Thompson	$2.75
☐	40927-1	**Slumber Party** Christopher Pike	$2.50
☐	41186-1	**Son of Interflux** Gordon Korman	$2.50
☐	41513-7	**The Tricksters** Margaret Mahy	$2.95
☐	41546-8	**Yearbook II: Best All-Around Couple** Melissa Davis	$2.50

PREFIX CODE
0-590-

Available wherever you buy books...
or use the coupon below.